'A man can only take so much, Candra.' Simeon's smile faded abruptly.

'And so can a woman,' she snapped.

'Some man hurt you? It's not simply because you don't agree with what I'm doing, it's because I'm a man. It's *me* you object to.'

'Don't flatter yourself.'

'But you also realise you're fighting a losing battle.'

'And what is that supposed to mean?' Candra frowned.

He smiled and ran the backs of his fingers gently down her cheek. 'This.'

Candra swallowed hard, but she could not ignore the leaping of her pulse.

'Maybe it pleases you to deny feeling a response,' he went on, his narrowed blue eyes penetrating through her clothes to her heated skin beneath, 'but feel it you did. Maybe I'll be the one to make you forget all about your ambition, and you'll become truly a woman.'

TRAPPED

BY

MARGARET MAYO

MILLS & BOON LIMITED
ETON HOUSE   18-24 PARADISE ROAD
RICHMOND   SURREY   TW9 1SR

*First published in Great Britain 1990
by Mills & Boon Limited*

© Margaret Mayo 1990

*Australian copyright 1990
Philippine copyright 1990
This edition 1990*

ISBN 0 263 76743 4

*Set in Times 11 on 12½ pt.
01 – 9007-48910*

Typeset in Great Britain by JCL Graphics, Bristol

Made and printed in Great Britain

CHAPTER ONE

CANDRA strode between the derelict warehouses, her heavy corn-coloured hair in its pageboy bob swinging from side to side, a big brown leather bag on one shoulder, a nylon suitcase in her hand. Her holiday in Spain had been totally enjoyable, but she was glad to be back. Ahead of her bounded Skye and Lady, also happy to be home.

Her first glimpse of the canal brought a smile to her lips; she loved her new home on the water. How tranquil it was, this cutting that ran through England. Once used for transporting coal, sand and other commodities, now much used by holiday boats in a booming leisure industry. Behind her was the growing Staffordshire town of Stonely, but here, scarcely a hundred yards away, was a different world—a world of beauty, a world of nature, a world where time stood still.

A frown took the place of Candra's smile when she saw that a lot of the boats were missing. Her neighbours often went off for the day or the week, or a month even, but so many at the same time? That was unheard of.

She stood a moment and studied the empty mooring spaces, and even the dogs seemed to sense that there was something wrong, nuzzling her hand, looking up at her with their soft brown eyes. 'I expect there's some perfectly logical explanation,' she told them.

Candra spoke to her dogs as though they were humans. Her parents had not liked the idea of her living here alone; her father in particular had objected most strongly. He'd said she would be too vulnerable, and had only relented when she agreed to take the two dogs with her. And what good company they had proved to be.

''Ad a good 'oliday, Candra?'

She turned her head at the sound of the voice. 'Very good, thank you, George.' A head and shoulders emerged from one of the boats, a shining, tanned bald head with a fringe of grey hair. Watery blue eyes looked at her through a network of wrinkles. George Miller was retired now, but he had worked canal boats all his life. He wore a white collarless shirt and braces, and a pipe hung permanently in one corner of his mouth.

'Things 'ave been 'appenin',' he said glumly.

'So I see.' She walked to him and set down her case. 'Where are they all?'

He lifted bony shoulders. 'Gone.'

'What do you mean, gone?' She frowned. 'Where? Why?'

'Orders.'

Her frown deepened. 'What are you talking about, George? Whose orders?'

'We got this notice. Can't do anythin' about it. Came the day you went.'

'What notice? What did it say?' insisted Candra. 'Who sent it?'

'Best read it,' he advised. A suspicion of tears moistened his eyes, and he disappeared below.

Candra climbed on to *Four Seasons*, her own green-painted boat with the panels of pretty seasonal flowers decorating the sides, unlocked the double doors and pushed back the slide over the hatch. The dogs raced down the steps in front of her, scattering the mail, sniffing excitedly, making sure nothing had changed. They had been looked after by Candra's parents while she was away.

A quick scan of the envelopes told her that there was no notice here. She puzzled over it while she filled the kettle and lit the gas stove, but as she bent to pick up the dogs' water bowl Candra spotted a sheet of paper that had slid partly beneath a cupboard.

As she read the typewritten words it all became clear. But he couldn't do it. She wouldn't let him! After all the trouble her grandfather had gone to, ensuring nothing like this happened, he was calmly telling them that he was going to build a marina and convert the warehouses into a restaurant-cum-nightclub, that they would have to move their boats from the basin.

It was criminal! It was diabolical! She had known there was a possibility of some changes now the land was sold, but how dared—what was his name? She frowned down again at the piece of paper. Simeon Sterne. How dared Simeon Sterne assume he could get rid of them just like this? And why had the others given in to his demand? Why hadn't they stood united? If they didn't move, he couldn't go ahead with his development. It was as simple as that.

Candra's fingers strummed on the edge of the stove, the kettle whistled as it came to the boil, and the dogs barked as they always did when they heard the piercing noise. She turned the stove off and didn't stop to think twice. She was going to pay Simeon Sterne a visit.

She gave Skye a biscuit and left him to guard the boat, snapping her fingers to Lady and setting off back the way she had come. He was going to build a nightclub, was he? He was going to enlarge the canal basin and turn it into a marina. Probably with a fleet of hire-boats tied up where she and all the others had their homes. Over her dead body! Her grandfather had been a strong conservationist, and he'd had plans for this land when he owned it—and it certainly hadn't involved anything like this. It was her duty to uphold her grandfather's wishes.

By the time she reached the address on the letterhead, Candra's temper had reached boiling-point. This was her home and she loved it, and, apart from anything else, apart from what that damn man wanted to do, it was convenient to where she worked. She was not going to let anyone move her without a fight.

Sterne Developments' office block was new and impressive. A successful company by all accounts. It was not a firm she knew anything about. They were new in the area, having moved their offices from somewhere in the City.

She left Lady sitting outside, knowing the Alsatian would not budge until she herself gave the word. Candra's mood was not helped when she was told that Mr Sterne could not see her without an appointment. But she was determined not to go away. She wanted to see him—and she wanted to see him *now*! 'If you'd just give him my name, and tell him I own *Four Seasons*—it's a narrow-boat,' she added in response to the girl's frown. 'I think you'll find that he'll see me.'

His secretary looked doubtful, but she rang through all the same, and after a few seconds' conversation she nodded. 'Mr Sterne has someone with him at the moment, but he'll see you if you care to wait? Would you like a cup of coffee?'

'No, thanks,' replied Candra tersely.

'Please sit down,' invited the girl.

Candra obeyed, but could not relax. With one eye on the clock and one on his door, she went over what she was going to say. He would find that she was not so meek and mild as the rest of the boat owners. If only she hadn't been away! They could have all got together and fought this man. She'd already had some right royal battles with other firms interested in building on parcels of land her grandfather had owned, but this was by far the most preposterous development.

The minutes ticked away as she sat and waited. They turned to half an hour, then an hour, and just when she was contemplating storming into his office the door opened.

Simeon Sterne had intense blue eyes and stood well over six feet. He wore a dark grey suit which sat handsomely on broad shoulders, and a white silk shirt. He smiled as he shook the hand of his visitor, but the other man's face was set in grim, angry lines, as though the outcome of their meeting had not been to his satisfaction. Obviously Simeon Sterne was not an easy man to deal with.

When the blue eyes were turned on her there was nothing welcoming in them. They were utterly hard and cold, looking at her with intense dislike. A shiver ran down Candra's spine, but she straightened her shoulders and returned the stare haughtily.

'Miss Drake?' He held out his hand.

Candra ignored it and marched into his office. She heard his swift intake of breath as she passed him, and he closed the door with a resounding thud. It should have warned her, but she carried on regardless, turning swiftly around. 'Mr Sterne, I don't think I need spell out the reason for my visit. You do know why I am here?'

'Naturally.' He had thick black hair, so black as to be almost blue, brushed back off his tough, chiselled face. She judged him to be in his late thirties, and his bright piercing blue eyes looked at her and through her and told her that she was wasting her time. 'As a matter of fact, I've been expecting you.'

Candra frowned. 'You have?' And just for an instant she was taken back.

'You find that surprising?'

'Absolutely.'

'I'm only amazed it took you so long.'

'I don't know what you're talking about.'

An insolent smile curved his mouth. 'Lady, you have quite a reputation. Didn't you know that?'

'I have? In what way?' This man was throwing her off balance and she did not like it.

'I understand you're something of a conservationist?'

Her chin lifted. Now she knew what he was getting at. 'Maybe.'

'Quite a little battler when it comes to preserving your town's natural heritage, so I believe.'

'You think that's a bad thing?' she scorned with a flash of her grey-green eyes.

'It's admirable,' he said solemnly, but she knew he was mocking her. 'And now you've come to tell me what I should or should not be doing with the warehouse site.'

'That's right,' she snapped.

'Then feel free to go ahead.' With an amused smile, he walked over to his desk and leaned indolently back against it. He crossed one long leg over the other, pushed his hands into his trouser pockets, and looked totally relaxed, though Candra knew he was nothing of the sort. He was as wary as a jungle cat. He was poised to make his kill. He was playing with her!

Her anger deepened and she took a steadying breath before saying, 'Did you know my grandfather used to own that land?'

His thick black brows rose, and Candra could see that she had surprised him. 'As a matter of fact I didn't, but I don't see what difference it makes.'

'He intended pulling down the warehouses and turning the area into a nature reserve. He wanted to bring a breath of countryside right into the town and give the houses behind an uninterrupted view of the canal.'

'So why didn't he?'

'He died a few months ago.' Her eyes locked into his as she made the flat announcement, and the tension between them grew. Candra had tangled with a lot of officials in her recent fights against indiscriminate building; she had come up against a lot of tough-minded men, but none like this.

'And none of his family felt strongly enough about it to carry out his wishes?'

'Unfortunately, no,' said Candra. 'The land that my grandfather owned, and there was quite a lot of it, was left to my two uncles. All they were interested in was selling it off and making themselves some money.'

'Leaving you to fight the battles when building permission was sought?'

'That's right,' snapped Candra. 'My grandfather wanted Stonely to stay the cosy village it used to be. He was appalled when houses began to go up all over the place, and was determined he would never sell the land that he owned, not even if he were offered double or triple its value. My grandfather held very strong principles and——'

'You think that by charging in here and telling me all this you'll be able to change my mind?' he cut in peremptorily.

'If I don't, it won't be for want of trying,' she retorted. 'Don't you realise what you'll be doing to the people who live in the houses over the road from the warehouse site?'

'No one objected when my planning application was made,' he told her calmly. 'I think they're rather relieved that something's going to be done after all these years. It can't have been very pleasant looking out at derelict buildings.'

'And it won't be very pleasant when the streets are filled with loud-mouthed drunks at two o'clock in the morning.'

The blue eyes glittered. 'I think, Miss Drake, that you have the wrong conception. It will be a very high-class restaurant and an exclusive nightclub. No trouble, no noise.'

'No?' she asked, fine brows rising. 'You don't think that you'll attract customers from the marina? Holiday-makers out for a good time?'

'Since the marina is solely for the hire of boats, and customers will simply come and go, I don't see that the problem will arise,' he answered her coolly. 'But I think maybe we're getting to the real truth of the matter.' He paused and looked at her, and Candra felt the full impact of that icy gaze. 'It's the marina development that bothers you. The fact that you're being asked to move.'

'I admit that is a factor,' she returned with equal

frostiness. 'A very important one.'

'It's no place for a girl alone— or perhaps you don't live alone? I see you're not married; do you have a resident boyfriend?'

Candra's chin lifted. 'What is this, Mr Sterne, an interrogation into my private life?'

He shrugged. 'Your private life is of no interest to me whatsoever.'

'You're simply interested in getting rid of my home?' she asked abruptly.

'Your boat, Miss Drake, and you still haven't told me why it took you so long to come and see me. No, don't tell me, let me guess. With that perfect tan you must have been on holiday. Was it somewhere nice? Did you enjoy it?'

His condescending tone incensed Candra. He was no more interested in where she had been than in listening to her demands that he forget his project. 'I got back a few hours ago,' she spat, 'and you can imagine my astonishment when I found out what had been happening while I was away. The other boat owners should have banded together and told you exactly what you could do with your fancy ideas.'

'Believe me, they tried,' he informed her. 'But it didn't make any difference.'

Because most of them were retired couples seeking only a peaceful existence. 'Where have they gone?' she demanded bluntly.

'I didn't ask.'

'And you don't care?'

'I imagine they've found other perfectly good moorings. It shouldn't be too difficult.'

'But not near here,' she insisted. 'There are no other

residential moorings within miles, and for your information, Mr Sterne, I happen to like it here. I don't have far to travel to work, it's reasonably near my parents, and I don't see why any of use should move just because you want to develop the site.'

'You're forgetting,' he grated, 'that I don't intend to accommodate residential boats.'

'Are you saying that we could leave them there if we didn't live on them?'

'Something like that, yes,' he shrugged, 'once the work's finished. Meanwhile you and everyone else will have to move.'

'And if we refuse?'

He sighed impatiently. 'Then I shall obviously take legal action. Now, if you've quite finished, please go. Unless——' a sudden thought struck him '—you're not capable of handling the boat? I never thought about that. You only live on it, don't you? You probably never go anywhere. Would you like me to move it for you?'

His patronising manner infuriated Candra, and she threw him a look designed to kill. 'I was handling boats as soon as I was out of nappies. If you don't believe me, come along some time and I'll give you a demonstration.'

His smile failed to reach his eyes. 'I'll come and watch when you leave, Miss Drake. Do be sure to invite me.'

'You'll wait a long time for that,' she tossed back smartly. 'I have no intention of moving, *ever*. Do I make myself clear?'

Simeon Sterne had full lips, but at this moment they clamped together until they were almost invisible. 'I shall be perfectly within my rights, Miss Drake, when the time comes, in having you moved. Don't make me do it.'

Candra realised that she could go on arguing until doomsday and he would not change his mind. He was totally implacable. And she could see why some of the other boat owners had already given in and gone. The rest would undoubtedly follow.

'You've not heard the last of this,' she told him boldly. 'There has to be something I can do.'

'That's your prerogative, lady, but I fear you'll be wasting your time. I've had full planning permission, both from British Waterways and the local council. You don't have a leg to stand on.'

Candra glared. 'We'll see about that.' And with her head held high she turned and marched out of his office.

Lady sensed her mistress's mood and walked sedately at her heel. Even when they reached the warehouses, where she usually bounded on ahead, the dog continued to pad along at Candra's side, looking up at her questioningly.

'It's all right, girl.' Candra patted her head. 'I'm just angry, so angry. That rat has no soul. But he's not going to win. It's just a matter of working it out.'

That night Candra dreamt about Simeon Sterne, of piercing blue eyes and an unsmiling mouth, of a tall, rangy body and tanned, long-fingered hands, and she awoke with him still in her thoughts. Her anger had not abated.

She let the dogs out, then showered and dressed, and all the time her mind ran on ahead. She was furious that she had not heard about the development in time to voice her protest. It actually looked as though there was nothing she could do. But she sure as hell could make things difficult for him. Like absolutely refusing to move. And maybe she could get some of the others to do the same.

Buying this boat had meant independence. For twenty-seven years she had lived under her parents' roof —and under her father's thumb! Her friends had told her she should have got out a long time ago, but love and loyalty had kept her tied. Then promotion twelve months earlier had brought a substantial increase in salary—and this boat had come up for sale! It was the incentive she needed.

Owning a boat and actually living on it had been a dream for a long time. She'd had many holidays afloat as a child, and her father—and his father and grandfather before him—had actually worked boats for a living. Naturally her father had been very much against the idea, but for once she had stood firm, and during the last year Candra's confidence had grown out of all recognition.

Her new job as company secretary was demanding, and she found *Four Seasons* an ideal place to unwind after a hectic day's work. Now Simeon Sterne had disturbed her peace of mind, and instead of going back to the office relaxed and refreshed she was filled with burning anger and the certain knowledge that she would have to move in the end.

Candra had no opportunity to think about her problems on her first day back. In fact she worked late, catching up on all that had accumulated while she was away. By the time she got home and cooked a meal, exercised the dogs, and spent a few minutes chatting to George Miller, telling him about her interview with Simeon Sterne, it was time to go to bed.

The next few days followed a similar pattern, and Candra came no nearer to finding a solution. She rang a solicitor friend who told her that there was absolutely nothing she nor any of the other boat owners could do. If Simeon Sterne had already obtained permission, he could not be stopped, and he would be perfectly within his rights to move them once he was ready to start work.

More of the boats left, despite Candra's efforts to get them to band together. It was very disappointing. She could see the time coming when only George and herself remained. George was as stubborn as she, but for very different reasons. He had lived here all his life, not in this exact spot, but not far away, and he wanted to die here. It was as simple as that.

On Saturday Candra held a dinner party. Her dinners were always a huge success and she enjoyed the challenge of creating them on her tiny gas stove. Everyone loved the novelty of dining on a narrowboat.

Today she was entertaining Liz, an old friend from her schooldays, and her husband, Dave, and Andrew Roland, who was a buyer at the same company where she worked. He was divorced, in his early thirties, and frequently asked her out. But after Craig, who had been as bad as her father for trying to rule her life, she was not interested in a committed relationship. She intended concentrating solely on her career.

Andrew arrived first. He was a tall, thin, fairly serious individual, with gold-rimmed glasses and receding mousy-brown hair. He took one look at her and beamed. 'Candra, you look delightful.'

She wore a yellow and white silk dress and large gold hoop earrings. Living on a boat did not mean that she had to slop around in jeans all the time. Candra always dressed well, even when she was not entertaining.

He accepted the glass of sherry she offered, patted the dogs who were jostling for attention, and they moved into her cosy little lounge with its shining brasses and crisp lace curtains. 'What's happened to all the other boats?' he asked with a frown as he sat down on one of the pink Dralon seats. 'I was amazed to see how many of them had gone.'

'I wish you hadn't asked,' said Candra fiercely. 'It's a sore point.'

His brows rose. 'But since I have asked, I'd like an answer. I've always thought you were vulnerable here, but even more so now.'

'You sound like my father,' said Candra sharply.

'He's a sensible man.'

'Actually,' she admitted, 'we've had our marching orders. There are going to be some changes around here.'

'Such as?'

'A proper marina, a restaurant-cum-nightclub.'

He frowned. 'Who's developing it?'

'A hateful individual by the name of Simeon Sterne.'

'Of Sterne Developments?' And when she nodded, 'I've heard of them. They're making quite a name for themselves. Where are you moving to?'

'That,' said Candra bitterly, 'is the sixty-four-thousand-dollar question. I don't want to go. I intend fighting him tooth and nail.'

'I wish you luck,' said Andrew. 'From what I've heard, he's a pretty ruthless character.'

'You don't have to tell me. I've already had one confrontation with him.'

He grinned. 'And I imagine sparks flew?'

'I've had enough of people walking all over me,' she said sharply. 'Here's Liz and Dave, excuse me a moment.'

Her friends, too, were concerned by what was going on, and a lot of the conversation that evening centred on Simeon Sterne, and where Candra could move to if she was finally forced to go.

Liz was a bubbly blonde, and Dave had red hair and a temper to match. Their marriage was anything but placid, but they were happy all the same.

It was a beautiful early summer evening, and was still fairly light when they were sitting in her lounge, drinking their coffee and sipping Rémy Martin. Candra took a casual glance out of the window and saw a shadowy figure approaching. 'You're not going to believe this, everyone,' she said quietly, 'but Simeon Sterne is walking towards the boat at this very moment.'

'Where? Where?' Liz eagerly craned for a glimpse of him. 'Oh, Lord, is that him? He's nothing like I imagined. He's so tall, so good-looking, so——'

'Liz!' threatened her husband.

She grimaced wryly. 'A pity he's the enemy. Do you think, Candy, that he's come to talk to you? Will we be in the way? Ought we to go?'

'Don't you dare!' cried Candra. 'But if you'll excuse me for a moment I'll go and see what he wants. Watch the dogs for me.' She hurried through the dining area where dirty dishes still sat on the table, and through the galley where more plates were waiting to be washed, and up the steps to the stern deck. He was standing there, still dressed in a dark suit and white shirt, still looking as forbidding as she remembered, though the dusk softened the hardness of his features.

'I take it,' she said coldly, 'that you've come to see whether I'm still here?' The few inches' height the boat gave her brought her face on a level with his, and she gazed fearlessly at him.

'That was the idea, yes.' His eyes raked her body, not missing one inch of her anatomy, everything from her high-heeled white sandals and her long slender legs to the flatness of her stomach, from her trim waist to the firm thrust of her breasts, and she wouldn't have been human if she hadn't felt a tingle of response. But it was squashed immediately, and he continued his long, slow appraisal, over he wide mouth and tip-tilted nose, right up to the shiny gloss of her hair. 'You seem to be having a bit of a party,' he commented. 'A last farewell, is it?'

'No way,' she answered bluntly, resenting the way he had looked at her.

He frowned. 'You're not ready to move?'

'Not now, not ever, Didn't I make myself clear?'

His eyes hardened and narrowed. 'Really, Miss Drake, why do you insist on making things difficult for yourself?'

'The only way you'll move me is by force,' she told him strongly. 'And you'll have to get a warrant to do that, otherwise I'll prosecute you for trespassing.'

A thick black brow arched, but he said nothing. Instead he stepped back and let his eyes rove over the boat—as they had her earlier. Autumn and winter were the scenes depicted on the side nearest him. Holly and mistletoe, a robin and Christmas roses. Russet beech leaves and ears of corn, berries and nuts, a tiny doormouse. 'It's a nice boat. Did you do the paintings yourself?'

Candra shook her head. 'The previous owner did.'

'I wonder he could bear to sell. What's it like inside?'

'If you're after an invitation, forget it,' she said sharply.

'I wouldn't dream of disrupting your party. Do you entertain often?'

'I don't think I like all these questions, Mr Sterne. If all you came for was to find out whether I'd moved, then you have your answer. Please go.'

'I may have found you somewhere,' he said.

Candra's eyes shot wide. 'Your kindness overwhelms me,' she scorned. 'But no, thanks. I happen to prefer it here.'

'A friend of mine has a house with some land running down to the canal,' he went on, as though she had not spoken. 'He's willing to let you live on your boat there.'

'I cannot believe this,' she said. 'Have you made similar offers to all the other boat owners? Have you gone around trying to fix them all up?'

'Only you.'

Candra frowned. 'Why have I been singled out for special treatment?'

'Because, dear lady, you are the only one who's giving me a hard time.'

'Mr Miller isn't going to move either.'

'Mr Miller? *Black Princess*. That's his boat next to yours, isn't it?'

She nodded.

'Have you put him up to it?' His tone was harsh as he rapped the question.

'No, I have not,' she answered heatedly. 'George Miller has lived and worked on the canal all his life. He was born and bred in Stonely, and he wants to spend the rest of his days here. If you've a heart at all in that stone-cold body of yours, then spare a thought for him.'

His brows drew together harshly, his mouth grew grim. 'I don't need you to tell me what to do, Miss Drake.'

'And I don't need you to help me. But, as a matter of interest, how much pressure did you exert on your friend? He doesn't know me, or what I'm like. I could have lots of rowdy friends, for all he knows. And besides, I wouldn't want to intrude on his privacy. To keep a boat you need free access to it, not across someone's garden. And my dogs, they need exercise—would he like it if they ran about his property?'

'Dogs?' He frowned.

'Yes, that's right, dogs. I have two savage Alsatians who guard me and my boat with their life.' As if on cue, Skye came up the steps, and the instant he saw a strange man he began barking. Candra checked him and he stopped, but he growled and bared his teeth, looking totally unapproachable, although Candra knew Skye would not hurt Simeon Sterne unless he attempted to touch her boat.

'I can see why you're not afraid here on your own,' he admitted.

'And I imagine you can see why I couldn't take your friend up on his offer—even if I considered moving—which I'm not,' she hastened to add.

'You're a fool,' he grated.

His aggressive tone registered with Skye, who began barking again, and Andrew came up the steps to see what was going on. 'Candra, is this man troubling you?' He put his arm protectively about her shoulders, though Candra could not dismiss an inner smile. Andrew was as tall as Simeon, but physically there was no comparison. Even in his suit there was no disguising Simeon's breadth of shoulder and powerful arms and legs. In contrast, Andrew was a puny weakling.

'He's just leaving,' she said.

Simeon's flint-like eyes rested on the other man. 'As you seem to be a very close friend of Miss Drake, perhaps you can persuade her that she's making a big mistake? I have no intention of backing down on this issue, but neither do I want an ugly confrontation.' With that he swung on his heel and marched back the way he had come.

'He certainly doesn't believe in mincing words, does he?' asked Andrew when they descended back into the boat. 'But he's right, you know. You really should move.'

'I resent being told what to do.'

'I'll come and help you look for somewhere tomorrow, if you like——?'

'What's happened?' interrupted Liz, looking from one to the other with interest. 'Was that what he came for, to insist once again that you move?'

Candra nodded. 'And he actually said that he had found me somewhere. Can you believe his audacity?'

'It sounds as though he's being helpful,' said Liz.

'Because it's in his own interest,' Candra snapped.

'So you turned down his offer?'

'You bet I did.'

Liz looked significantly at her husband. 'The girl's crazy.'

'I know what I'm doing.' Candra glared at her.

'I think we should go,' said Dave.

Candra nodded. 'Simeon Sterne's ruined a good

evening, I'm sorry.'

'Don't apologise,' he smiled. 'Let's just thank our lucky stars he didn't come earlier. The food was excellent, as always. Thanks a lot, Candra. I'd invite you to our house, but you know what a rotten cook Liz is.'

Liz poked him in the ribs. 'You eat it.'

'Only because I have no choice.'

Their good-natured bantering carried on as they stood up and made their way off the boat. Andrew followed reluctantly. 'Would you like me to stay and keep you company for a while?' he asked. 'I'll help wash up. I don't fancy leaving you in this state.'

But Candra shook her head. 'You know I never allow my guests to wash up. Don't worry about me, I'll be fine.'

He looked doubtful, but accepted it. 'You will let me come tomorrow?'

'If you like,' she said, 'but I'm not so sure about hunting for moorings. I don't want to move.'

'You'll have to in the end,' he told her kindly. 'It will do you no harm to look.'

'I suppose so,' she admitted, 'but I'm not going to rush it. There's plenty of time. Let Sterne have a few headaches first. He's a swine. I hate him.'

After Andrew had gone Candra let the dogs out while she washed up, then as soon as everywhere was neat and tidy she went to bed.

Her bedroom was in the fore-end of the boat, a permanent one, so there was no struggling to make it up each evening. It was tiny but practical, with a light over the bed, a bookshelf, wardrobe and mirror. The walls were clad in pine, as was the whole boat, and her duvet was sunshine-yellow. It was a cheerful room, especially first thing in the morning when sunlight streamed through the window.

But Candra was not feeling particularly cheerful tonight. Simeon Sterne had put a damper on things and she found it difficult to dismiss him from her thoughts. She resented him, she resented his whole attitude, and she knew that until she actually moved he would continue to harass her.

Maybe she ought not to have been so eager to dismiss his friend's offer. It could be a solution. On the other hand, he had not said how far away it was. She liked being close to her work. It was nice having a brisk walk to the office each morning instead of driving through heavy traffic and having frayed nerves.

Eventually sleep claimed her, and on Sunday morning the sun was shining, the birds were singing, and it was impossible to be down-hearted. She fed the dogs and then herself, and Andrew turned up at ten-thirty.

They had lunch at a pub and had a very pleasant day, but they could find no moorings for her boat. 'It looks to me,' said Andrew, 'as though you'll have no choice but to accept Sterne's friend's offer.'

'I'll find somewhere,' she said, 'when I'm good and ready.' Though she could see it was not going to be easy, and again she felt resentment towards Simeon Sterne for causing this problem.

'Thanks for taking me out,' she said to Andrew when they returned a little after four. 'I've really enjoyed it.'

She got out of his car, and he wanted to walk through the derelict warehouse site with her, but she would not let him. When she got to *Four Seasons*, however, she began to wish that she had. The doors were open, the slide pushed back, and there was no sign at all of the dogs.

CHAPTER TWO

CANDRA'S heart banged against her ribcage as she took the last few steps towards *Four Seasons*. She could hear nothing and see no one—but someone had been there, might even still be inside! Someone had unlocked her boat—and had miraculously done it without being attacked by her dogs. Unless—the horrifying thought sickened her and fear caught in her throat, but the next second Lady sprang up the steps, almost knocking her over in her eagerness. Candra's relief knew no bounds. 'Oh, Lady, *Lady*, thank goodness you're safe. What's going on? Where's Skye?'

She moved to the doorway as she spoke, and looked down into the kitchen. In the cabin beyond she could see a man's polished shoe, and Skye standing close. A deep frown grooved her brow. 'Skye?' she called. 'Here, boy.'

But, although the dog looked at her and wagged his tail, he made no attempt to move, and then the man stepped into view and she could see that Skye's collar was being held by a firm, long-fingered, brown hand.

'*You*!' she accused, climbing down into the boat and meeting the cool blue eyes of the intruder. 'What are you doing here? How did you get in? And how did you pacify the dogs? They never let anyone on board.'

Simeon Sterne indolently lifted his shoulders. 'They obviously made an exception in my case.'

He looked relaxed and perfectly at home, and certainly the dogs were friendly enough, fussing around

26

him as though he were a regular visitor to *Four Seasons*. He wore light blue trousers today, and a knitted silk half-sleeved shirt which accentuated the muscular power only hinted at beneath his tailored suits.

'I can't understand it,' she said. 'It's a wonder they didn't tear a piece out of your arm. But, in any case, you had no right breaking in.'

'I did not force your lock, Miss Drake,' he said firmly. 'The boat was open. Therefore I decided you couldn't be far away and I thought I'd sit and wait.'

Candra frowned. She always locked her boat, no matter how short a time she intended being absent. He was lying—and he was a big man in this tiny cabin. He filled it with his presence. It had never felt so claustrophobic before.

'I must admit,' he went on, 'that I didn't expect so long a wait.'

'Why don't I believe you?' she enquired acidly. 'I always, always lock my boat.'

'Not today you didn't.'

Candra cast her mind back and suddenly realised that he was right. When Andrew arrived, eager to get going, she had closed the doors but hadn't checked them. And earlier she had slid the catch down on the Yale lock so that the dogs would not bang the door closed and lock her out. They had done that more than once.

He was watching her closely and saw the realisation dawn. It did not please Candra to be caught out like this, and she turned away angrily. 'You had no right making yourself at home, none at all.' He seemed much taller and broader here, and she could smell his musky aftershave and feel his masculinity. He posed a threat which she did not like.

'Would you have preferred me to stand around waiting outside?'

'I'd rather you'd gone away and not come back,' she snapped.

'The dogs were lonely. I thought I'd keep them company.'

Candra could still not understand how easily they had made friends, and it definitely made her feel less secure. If they had taken to Simeon Sterne so readily, they could take to anyone. A cold shiver ran down her spine.

'Perhaps you'd like to tell me exactly why you are here?' she asked coldly.

Black brows slid up. 'Isn't it obvious? We were interrupted last night. I came to finish our conversation.'

'As far as I'm concerned, it was finished,' she rasped.

Undaunted, he said, 'Can I take it that you've been out searching for new moorings?'

'As a matter of fact, yes,' she admitted tightly, reluctantly.

He looked pleased. 'So you've come to your senses? You've realised that being stubborn will get you nowhere?'

'No, I have not,' she flung back crossly. 'I still do not and never will approve of what you are going to do. I shall do everything within my power to stop it.'

'But you must realise it's inevitable, otherwise you wouldn't have gone out looking for alternative moorings.'

'It was merely a way of passing a Sunday afternoon,' she snapped, hating the note of triumph in his voice. 'But it was a waste of time; we found nothing. I shan't bother again.'

'We?' He frowned.

Candra did not see what business it was of his whom she had been with, so she glared coldly and said nothing.

'I take it you're referring to your friend from last night? Where is he now? Surely he wasn't ungallant enough to let you come back to an empty boat alone?'

His mockery increased Candra's anger, and she turned on him savagely. 'Mr Sterne, I'd appreciate it if you'd get off my boat. You're not welcome here—now—or ever.'

But he stood firm. 'Not until I'm satisfied that you're going to move.'

'I might, when I'm good and ready,' she told him loftily. 'But certainly not until I've done everything I can to get your project stopped.'

'Miss Drake,' he said impatiently, 'surely you realise that you're fighting a losing battle? There is nothing that you or anyone can do now.' After a moment's pause he went on, 'My friend's offer still stands. The dogs are no problem.'

Surprised by his sudden change of direction, Candra frowned. 'You've asked him?'

'It will be all right,' he insisted.

'I'll bear it in mind,' she said, adding scornfully, 'as a last resort.'

His mouth tightened. 'I seem to be wasting my time.'

'I'm glad you realise it.'

He stared at her long and hard, and there was no escaping the penetrating depths of his blue eyes. Candra had never encountered eyes like these before. They were hypnotic; she couldn't look away. It was as though he was looking right into her mind, reading it, knowing every little thing that was going on.

She shifted uncomfortably, but still his eyes held

hers, until with a last impatient shake of his head he swung on his heel and left. The boat rocked gently as he got off and Candra dropped on to a seat. In future she would double-check herself when she left the boat, and if that man dared to put foot on it she would—she would push him into the canal.

She ate a light supper of wholemeal bread sandwiches filled with chopped boiled egg and mayonnaise, walked the dogs, and then went to bed. But not to sleep. She kept imagining Simeon Sterne in her boat. No matter how she tried, the thought would not go away. In the end she got up and heated some milk, sipping until it warmed and soothed her. Even so, it was almost daybreak before she finally dropped off.

When the alarm shrilled she groaned and put her head under the duvet. She was tired. She did not want to get up. And then she remembered the reason she was tired, and she sprang crossly out of bed.

As she showered and dressed she could not help but wonder whether he would come back and tyrannise her further, or would he let matters take their course? Would he actually take the threatened legal action if she did not move? She decided that, yes, he would. He was that type of man.

When Candra got home from work that evening another two boats had moved. It left only her and George. 'What are you going to do about it?' she asked him.

The old man shrugged. 'Reckon I'll 'ave to go. Don't want to.'

'Of course you don't,' she said gently. 'You must fight him. He must be made to see that he can't do this to us.'

'Too old to fight,' he mumbled.

'But I'm not,' she said sharply. 'I'll do all I can, George, rest assured about that.'

'Might 'ave to sell.'

'Oh, no, please don't say that.'

'Nowhere else to go.'

She nodded sadly. 'I know. I tried yesterday to find somewhere and couldn't. But I shan't give up. I wish I'd been here when he'd dished those notices out. We could have banded together and refused point-blank to move.'

George shook his head, as much as to say it wouldn't have got them anywhere. And he was probably right.

Candra moved on to her own boat and let out the dogs. They were very good when they were shut in, never showing any sign of distress. They were brother and sister, and their mother had belonged to Candra's parents too. She left the windows open and plenty of fresh water, and George let them out at lunchtime. They were never any trouble. Indeed, they were excellent guard dogs. Except where Simeon Sterne was concerned!

Candra still puzzled over how easily he had made friends with them. It had never happened before. Obviously he had some likeable quality, though she had yet to discover it.

Even before she reached her boat the next evening after work, Candra could see Simeon Sterne standing by it. Her heart sank. What did he want now? But when she got closer she discovered that he was not by *Four Seasons* at all. He was talking to George Miller.

She knew what he was doing. He had come to speak to George the same as he had her. To make sure that he was going to move. Her blood boiled and she hastened her steps. But before she got there the old man disappeared back into his boat and Simeon moved away, seeming surprised to see her when he turned.

'Good evening, Miss Drake.' The cool blue eyes rested on her.

Candra nodded curtly. 'I hope you haven't been upsetting Mr Miller?'

'I don't think so.'

'He's a dear old man and he's worried sick. He's even talking about selling his boat so that he doesn't have to move out of Stonely, and that would break his heart.'

'I'm sure something will come up.'

'You've no idea,' she spat, 'how difficult you're making life for us.'

His black brows rose. 'That was never my intention.'

'No?' she scorned. 'You're so damned full of what you want to do that you don't care about us. Well, I care. I care about myself, and I care about Mr Miller. Just go away, Mr Sterne. Go to hell.'

His lips pursed disapprovingly. 'And I thought you were a lady.'

'How can I be when I've got a swine like you on my back?' she demanded.

'Nevertheless, you have spirit, and I like that. Can I take you out to dinner tonight?'

Candra could not believe he was asking this of her. 'You have a nerve. What are you hoping to do? Ply me with drink so that I won't know what I'm saying and agree to move to your friend's place?'

He smiled wryly. 'Do you know what, Miss Drake? I don't think you would ever allow yourself to get drunk. From what I can see you always like to be in total control of yourself.'

'Too true I do,' she snapped.

'Let me guess what you do for a living.' He stroked his chin as he deliberated. 'You obviously like to be in charge. A teacher, perhaps? No?' as she shook her head. 'You own a boutique, then? Or should I say a very classy dress shop, judging by the clothes that you wear?'

'Wrong again, Mr Sterne.' Though she had to admit the compliment pleased her. 'As a matter of fact, Mr Sterne, I'm company secretary for Thorag Pharmaceuticals.'

'I'm impressed.'

'And I plan to be on the board before I'm thirty.'

'Admirable.'

Candra sensed he was mocking her, and her eyes flashed, more green than grey at this moment in time. 'I'm serious.'

'I don't doubt it.'

'You don't look as though you believe it to me,' she snapped. 'Or is it that you don't approve of women in business?'

He smiled. 'I have my views. Shall we discuss them over dinner?'

Candra was tempted. He was exhilarating company, if nothing else. The evening would certainly not be dull. But it would be an unwise move. She saw George looking at them through his window, and she shook her head. 'No, thank you.'

'That's a pity. I would have enjoyed it.'

'I can't think why.'

'It would be stimulating.'

'Meaning we would argue all the time?' she asked crossly.

'Not at all. We could have a healthy discussion. We could each air our opinions.'

'I don't think I could ever air my opinions with you, Mr Sterne, without sparks flying.'

He seemed amused. 'How will you ever find out what I'm like if you don't give yourself the chance?'

Candra shrugged. 'I don't particularly want to. Please excuse me, I must let my dogs out.'

She walked away from him, but he did not leave. He stood and watched while she unlocked, and when the Alsatians spotted him they jumped up and vied for his attention.

'Hello, Skye. Hello, Lady. So you remember me, eh? What a fussy pair you are. A pity your mistress isn't so friendly.'

'Nor would they be if they knew what you were up to,' shot Candra.

'I am merely doing what I have to do. Perhaps we can have dinner some other night, when you're in a more affable mood?'

Candra didn't even deign to answer. 'Goodbye, Mr Sterne.' And she swung herself down into the boat.

She was startled when he poked his head through the doorway. 'It's Simeon, Candra. Remember that in future, hmm?' With that he disappeared, and when she dared peep through the window he was nowhere in sight.

There was no doubt about it, she told herself angrily, Simeon Sterne had a cheek, he had an infernal cheek asking her to go out with him. Did he really think she would? He must have the hide of a rhinoceros. Couldn't he tell that she hated the sight of him? Didn't her words mean anything?

Oddly enough she saw nothing more of him. Whole days went by. The weekend. And still no sign. 'I don't like it,' she said to George Miller on Monday evening.

His tired thin shoulders lifted, and he chewed the end of his pipe. ''E's made 'is point. Can't do no more.'

'It's strange,' she frowned. 'I thought he'd be on our backs every day. Do you think he's cooking something up?'

Lips pursed and he shook his head.

'You're not on his side, are you?' she questioned caustically. George had never told her what Simeon had said that day she'd seen them talking together. But the old man was easily influenced. 'You don't condone what he's doing?'

'Man 'as to make a livin'.'

'But converting those warehouses after all the trouble my grandfather went to. The reason he purchased the land was so that nothing like this would happen. Stonely was such a lovely sleepy little place until they started expanding. Then they built all those houses and that industrial park, and now this. It's the beginning of the end, isn't it? And as for kicking us out of our homes, I think it stinks.'

'Time yet,' he said, 'to find somewhere. He did give us three months' notice.'

'I realise that,' she answered scathingly, 'but it doesn't alter the fact that there is nowhere else around here that is licensed for residential boats. We've got electricity, running water, toilet pump-out, everything. Lord, I hate that man.'

But if she was angry then, she was doubly so the next day when she discovered that the whole of the warehouse site had been cordoned off with wire fencing. Instead of short-cutting through it on her way home from work, she was compelled to use the road as far as the bridge and then walk along the side of the canal to the basin.

George was sitting on his foredeck when she arrived, sucking complacently at his pipe.

'What's going on? Why has he done that?' she wanted to know.

'Search me.'

'I shall find out.' But it would have to wait until morning. Simeon Sterne wouldn't be in his office now, and she didn't know where he lived. Candra was fuming.

Between the canal basin and the warehouses was a metre-high brick wall with an opening where many years ago had been a gate. This was also wired across. Every time Candra looked at it she felt like screaming.

But when morning came far more important matters needed her attention. She had risen early and walked the dogs, eaten a leisurely breakfast, and was in the middle of getting dressed when she heard the most blood-curdling sounds coming from inside the fenced area. Squeals of sheer pain and terror, as though someone were being murdered.

She shot out of the boat and across to the wall and the sight that met her eyes made her blanch. Lady was entangled in a coil of barbed wire, and the more she struggled, the more it cut into her. She was torn and bleeding, and crying and yelping and howling.

'*Oh, no*!' cried Candra, scrambling over the wall, as she did so calling to George, who was making his slow way towards her. 'Bring some wire-cutters, bring something. Lady's hurt. Oh, Lady, *Lady*!'

Skye stood nearby, obviously distressed, trying to get to Lady, but held back by the cruel barbs of the wire.

Candra could not get to her either. She tried, but the wire was too strong for her to separate, and as Lady moved it tore at Candra's hands. Lady was in too much pain to have the sense to keep still. She thrashed and struggled and made matters worse. 'Lady, please, please lie still,' implored Candra.

The dog looked at her with pain-filled eyes and for a moment did not move. 'That's a girl,' said Candra, reaching through the coils to pat her dog encouragingly. 'Easy now, easy does it.' But the next second Lady moved again and this time Candra's arm was caught in the wire.

'*George*!' she yelled. 'George, where are you?'

The old man looked over the wall, and his face was a picture when he saw the bloody scene. 'Go and fetch help,' she sobbed. 'The vet, a doctor, anyone. Quickly, George. Hurry.'

But George was too old to hurry. He was crippled with arthritis, so his steps were slow and painful, and Candra knew it would be quicker to drag herself free and fetch the vet herself, even though it meant tearing her arm to pieces.

She gritted her teeth and trying to hold the wire apart with one hand, slowly pulled back with her other. Lady for the moment had the good sense to stop wrestling, and finally, agonisingly, Candra was free.

Racing along the bank, she overtook George. 'Go back and keep your eye on Lady,' she panted.

At the pub under the bridge she pounded on the door until it opened. 'Mr Weston, please, I must use your phone,' and she pushed right past him.

'Of course, of course.' The tubby publican bustled after her. 'What's happened, has there been an accident?'

'My dog's stuck in some barbed wire. Oh, lord, I can't remember the vet's number. Do you know it?'

He nodded, and thankfully she got through straight away, explaining her problem, with panic in her voice. 'He's coming,' she said to the publican. 'I must get back now, thank you.' And she raced out again.

'But your arm, don't you think you ought to——' His concern was wasted. Candra was already out of earshot.

The vet arrived only minutes after Candra. By now Lady had exhausted herself, and lay on her side looking at her mistress with wide, soulful eyes, asking why she was not being rescued.

Candra's own eyes filled with tears and she couldn't bear to see Barry cutting the wire and pulling it out of Lady's skin, even though he had by now given her an injection.

'She won't feel it,' he assured Candra, but it didn't make her feel any better. Skye stood by whimpering, and Candra put her arms around him. George watched over the wall.

'How did this happen?' asked Barry, working quickly and skilfully, but even so he was unable to avoid getting scratched himself.

'I don't really know,' said Candra, 'but I imagine she jumped the wall and fell on it. They normally play in here, but yesterday Mr Sterne had this fence erected. He's going to redevelop the site.'

'And this barbed wire, I presume, was to go on top of the wall? Can't see much point in such a high fence otherwise.'

Candra shrugged. 'I don't know. I suppose so.'

Once the young vet had finished, he picked Lady up and carried her over the wall to his waiting car by the bridge. 'She'll need stitches,' he said. 'We'll keep her. You can fetch her tomorrow. And I suggest, Candra, that you get yourself off to the hospital.'

She looked down at her bleeding arm and nodded. 'Yes, I will.' But she had to see to Skye first. He was pacing backwards and forwards, already fretting for his sister. 'Come on, boy,' she said, patting him fondly. 'Let's get you back.'

George was hovering anxiously by the boats. 'Too old to 'elp. Sorry. 'Ow is she?'

'She'll be fine,' said Candra, trying to sound reassuring, though she did not feel it. 'They're keeping her overnight.'

'You're 'urt too.' He frowned.

She nodded. 'Will you keep an eye on Skye while I go to the hospital? But don't let him out, or he might go after Lady.'

George nodded. 'I'll 'ave 'im in my boat. 'E'll be all right. You get goin'.'

Candra's wounds were not deep enough to need stitching. They were cleaned and dressed, and she was given a tetanus injection, and could have easily gone to work. Instead she phoned from the hospital and told them not to expect her. There was one man she wanted to see, one man who was going to wish he had never heard the name Candra Drake.

She marched through the reception area at Sterne Developments, not looking to right or left, heading straight towards Simeon Sterne's suite of offices. His secretary looked up as Candra burst in, smiling when she recognised her, but when Candra strode right across to Simeon Stern's door, and it became obvious that she was going to walk in there too without knocking, her smile faced. 'Excuse me, but you can't go——'

'I can and I am,' said Candra firmly, the door already opening beneath her touch.

But her surprise attack was defeated when she found the office empty. Almost immediately, however, she heard the sound of papers being shuffled in an adjoining room. She smiled grimly to herself and moved towards his desk and waited.

On her previous visit she had given the room no more than a cursory glance, now she took the opportunity to look about her. It was vast to say the least, with a wide sweep of oatmeal carpet and hessian-covered walls hung with water-colours.

Pieces of antique furniture blended happily with modern. His huge oak desk with its wonderful patina of age was set at right angles to a window which almost filled one wall. Vertical blinds were angled to shut out the sun. His leather swivel-armchair was well worn and comfortable, but other chairs in the room were purely functional.

Along one wall was an enviable display of plants. Monstera Deliciosas with unbelievably glossy leaves, twining up towards the ceiling, aphelandra with its zebra-striped leaves, ficus elastica, ivies.

A sound behind caught Candra's attention. Simeon was moving towards her, his head bent over a sheet of paper. He wore navy trousers and a white shirt, no jacket. His sleeves were rolled up to his elbow, revealing sinewy arms with a covering of fine black hairs. His tie was loosened and the top button of his shirt undone.

'Mr Stern,' she said at once, her tone hard and angry.

He looked up with a frown, which changed immediately to a smile. 'Candra, how nice. My secretary didn't tell me you were here.'

'Because I didn't give her the chance,' she rasped.

'You wanted to surprise me? You've certainly done that. I never——Candra, you're hurt!' He broke off as he noticed her bandaged arm.

Her wide-spaced grey eyes flashed with loathing, and her freshly shampooed hair bounced healthily as she swung around to face him. 'This is nothing compared with what happened to Lady.' She was wearing a white blouse and a gored dogtooth checked skirt, the lining of which rustled as she moved. Her heels added another couple of inches to her five feet eight.

'To hell with your dog,' he said at once. 'It's you who concern me.'

'I bet I do,' she snapped. 'I bet you don't even realise that it's all your fault.'

A frown now gashed his forehead, and the grim lines about his mouth deepened. His blue eyes pierced hers. 'My fault, Candra? Mine? I'm sorry, but I haven't the slightest idea what you're talking about.'

'No?' she demanded scornfully. 'I'll tell you. But first of all you tell me why you put up that wire fencing.' She could afford to wait. She would play with him like a cat did a mouse.

'Why?' Black brows slid smoothly upwards. 'Isn't it obvious?' Blue eyes travelled the length of her body.

Candra tossed her head angrily. 'No, it is not obvious. All it means is that I have to go the long way round. Was that your idea? Make life difficult for me so that I'll be glad to move?'

'Now isn't that strange,' he said with a cynical smile, 'I never gave it a thought.'

'I bet!' she flung back scathingly. 'You must know I cut through there.'

'Regularly?'

'Regularly.'

'I'm sorry.'

'No, you're not,' she spat. 'It was a deliberate attempt to antagonise me.'

'An expensive one,' he said. 'Do you really think I'd go to all that trouble? The reason is simple. Vandals. Those warehouses are slowly being demolished brick by brick. I'd like something of them left before I begin my rebuilding programme.'

'How about the coils of barbed wire?' she slammed. 'What have you got in mind for them?'

He frowned. 'I gave orders for barbed wire to be put on top of the wall, but ——'

'They were not carried out,' cut in Candra sharply.

His eyes dropped again to her bandaged arm. 'Candra, you didn't—you haven't——?'

'That's right,' she interrupted icily, 'and Lady's being operated on right at this very moment. I hold you, Mr Sterne, responsible, and I want to know what you are going to do about it.'

CHAPTER THREE

SIMEON STERNE'S ice-blue eyes fixed steadily on Candra. 'Exactly where was the barbed wire?'

'What the hell does it matter where it was?' she yelled. 'Lady got caught up in it, and so did I, and I want to know what you're going to do about it.'

His frown deepened. 'Answer my question, dammit.'

Candra lifted her shoulders. 'The other side of the wall.'

'And how did you get in—through the gateway?'

She shook her head. 'That was fenced off too. But it makes no difference, you're responsible for it, and if Lady dies I shall take you to court.'

'She's that badly injured?' he wanted to know.

'Perhaps not,' she shrugged. 'Who's to say?'

'And you were in fact trespassing?' he questioned harshly.

Infuriated by the fact that he was trying to throw the onus on her, Candra shook her head, her eyes blazing. 'My dogs have always played on that site. But they're not human, Mr Sterne, they do not understand what a wire fence means. Lady jumped the wall and landed right in your barbed wire. I got this——' she held up her arm '—when I tried to rescue her. In the end I had to call the vet. If he hadn't come promptly, goodness knows what might have happened.'

'And you're blaming me?' There was not an ounce of sympathy in his voice.

'Of course I'm blaming you. It's entirely your fault.

That wire should never have been left lying around.'

'It was on my property. Your dog was in the wrong. And you were in the wrong for not controlling her.'

'I do not keep my eye on the dogs every second of the day,' blazed Candra. 'They're always out there when I'm at home. What do you expect me to do, tie them up?'

There were a few seconds' open hostility as Candra glared into the ice-cold blueness of his eyes. In all fairness, she knew it wasn't his fault, but at least he could show some compassion instead of this stone-cold, unfeeling, 'I'm in the right' attitude. She felt like spitting in his eye, or slapping him across the face, or doing something, anything, that would release the anger inside her.

'I'll take care of the vet's bill.'

'And you think that will solve everything?' she snapped. 'If you hadn't decided to build whatever it is you have in mind, this would never have happened.'

His tone was once again flint-like. 'I suggest you leave, Candra. Send me any bills, I'll see to them, but, as far as the development is concerned, it's still going through. And I'd like both you and George Miller to move on without further delay. The sooner you go, the sooner I can get started.'

Candra squared her shoulders and met the coldness of his eyes. She had come here prepared to do battle, and now he was turning out to be the victor. 'Correct me if I'm wrong, Mr Sterne, but you gave us three months' notice. I shall not move until the very last minute of the very last day, and if you think I'm being bloody-minded, then just look to yourself. Goodbye.'

She swung on her heel, and was almost out of the

office when his hand fell heavily on her shoulder. 'Just one moment, Candra,' he said, spinning her round to face him, 'there's something else. I cannot help but wonder whether you're as passionate in other ways as you are about this development.'

Candra frowned, then struggled furiously when it dawned on her what he was talking about. 'That, Mr Sterne, is something you're never likely to find out.'

'Is that so?' His hands slid from her shoulders to her back, moving her slowly but inexorably towards him.

'You swine!' she cried, trying without success to kick his shins. She ought to have guessed what was going to happen; she ought to have fought free long before this.

'Relax, Candra.' His voice was now soft and hypnotic. 'Watch you don't hurt your arm.'

As soon as her body was pressed completely against his, he lifted one hand up into the thickness of her hair and pulled her head back, so that she was compelled to look into his eyes. His other arm was in the small of her back and Candra could feel the whole hard length of him.

His heart was as erratic as her own, but she imagined it was for a very different reason. He was excited at the thought of kissing her; she felt nothing but stone-cold fury. If he thought he was going to soften her up this way, he was making a big mistake.

When his head lowered with that same unrelenting slowness, she used every atom of her strength to escape, but to no avail. And when his mouth closed on hers Candra felt a shudder run through her. She preferred to think it was revulsion, but knew in her heart of hearts that it was nothing of the sort. He was a very sensual man, and it was impossible not to respond.

Deliberately she held herself in check, wanting to show him that he had made a mistake. But when his mouth moved expertly over hers, when he ran the top of his tongue very gently over her clamped lips, when he turned his attention to other parts of her face, like the tip of her nose and the corners of her eyes, and behind her ears and in her ears, and beneath the heavy fall of her hair, then Candra felt herself relaxing.

Relaxing, but not responding. Accepting his kisses, but not returning them. She would never do that. He was employing emotional blackmail, and if he thought she couldn't see through his tactics, then he was blind.

But there was no escaping the fact that he was expert in what he was doing. Her heart thudded wildly, and she knew that if she wasn't careful she would end up kissing him. And that would be unthinkable.

To her relief, he lifted his head, even though he did not let her go. 'My congratulations.'

Candra frowned.

'How much longer could you have held out?' There was mockery now in his tone. 'Should I go on? Maybe if I . . .'

His mouth swooped on hers again, but this time Candra was ready for him. 'You swine!' she spat, finding sudden extra strength and breaking free. 'Do you really think I'd respond to you? If you want to know the truth, you make my skin crawl.'

'I think you're lying,' he grinned. 'To save your own face, perhaps? There's nothing wrong in feeling a good, healthy sexual response to a man.'

'There is when that man's you,' she retorted crossly.

'Simply because we have a difference of opinion where the building work is concerned, it doesn't mean to say that we can't be compatible in other ways.'

'Really?' she asked, brows arched in disdain. 'If that's the way you do business, then you've picked the wrong girl. I intend fighting you every inch of the way.'

'Attagirl,' he grinned, completely undaunted by her harsh words.

'I think you're doing a very lousy thing on my grandfather's land.'

'It's not your grandfather's any longer,' he reminded her.

'But you bought if from him,' she protested. 'At least, from my uncle. He should have told you what Grandad had in mind.He should never have let it go without stipulating that it was to be turned into a nature reserve.'

'Perhaps it's your uncle you should be telling all this to?'

Candra snorted derisively. 'He's as bad as you. All he wanted to do was make some quick money—and that's what you're after, isn't it?'

'It is the general reason why people go into business,' he answered smoothly.

'But a marina *and* a restaurant? Isn't that a bit extreme? I'm not in favour of either, but at least a marina wouldn't spoil anyone's view.'

'And hire-boats spend all the winter months being painted and maintained and earning no money,' he told her caustically. 'I want this area to be used. This is a growing town, Candra, and at the moment it's very short on amenities. I think you'll find it will be extremely popular. People like to sit and watch water, Candra. It's an ideal spot. I've been looking for somewhere like it for a long, long time.'

Candra tossed her head angrily. 'I might as well go,

I can see I'm getting nowhere.' He had an answer for everything, and, although she hated to admit it, she could see his point. But she would never agree, not in a thousand years; that would be letting her grandfather down.

She stalked across the room and opened the door, giving him one last haughty glance before she left. The fact that he was grinning all over his face added insult to injury, and she slammed the door shut with all her strength. With his secretary's astonished eyes on her, Candra walked from the office.

Outside the building, though, she leaned against the wall, her legs trembling so much that she could hardly stand. It was not so much their verbal battle that had drained her, but her unexpected response to Simeon's kiss.

For years now—ever since Craig died, in fact—she had kept her emotions rigidly in check. And now this man, this incredibly hateful man, was getting beneath her skin. And she did not know why. He was another one, like her father, like her brother, like Craig, who enjoyed giving orders, who only felt happy when they were manipulating other peoples lives, so why was he having this effect on her?

She puzzled over it as she made her way back to the boat. George Miller was looking out for her, and Skye raced forward, greeting her eagerly. 'You've been a long time,' George said worriedly.

Candra nodded. 'I went to see Mr Sterne when I came from the hospital. I wanted to tell him exactly what I thought of him for leaving that wire lying around.'

'It wasn't 'is fault,' frowned George.

'Which he didn't fail to point out,' she said harshly.

'But at least I got it out of my system.' The trouble was that she didn't feel any better for it. In fact, a whole new series of emotions had opened up.

''Ow's your arm?'

'Nothing serious, no stitches. It's Lady I'm worried about.'

'She'll be all right.'

Candra nodded. 'Perhaps I ought to go and see her?'

George took his pipe out of his mouth and shook his head. 'She'll be sedated. Best leave 'er alone.'

'I suppose so, but I'll phone anyway. I'll be back in a minute.'

She was reassured by Barry that Lady was being well looked after. 'She needed a fair number of stitches,' he said. 'Some of the cuts were pretty nasty. But they'll heal in no time. You've nothing to worry about, Candra. Come and fetch her in the morning.'

After lunch Candra took Skye for a long walk, right up to the lock a couple of miles away, and she stood watching as a boat approached. The lock was full, which meant that the holiday-makers had to wind the paddles open with a windlass to let out the water, reversing the procedure at the other end once they were in.

There was a white cottage by the lock which, in the canal's heyday, had belonged to the lock-keeper, and to her surprise it was up for sale. As she stood and looked at it, an idea dawned.

Candra's heart sang as she made her way back to *Four Seasons*. She wouldn't tell George yet; she'd find out the price. He had a beautiful boat worth many thousands, it should easily realise enough to buy the cottage. It would be perfect. And she could even tie up next to it herself!

She shut Skye in her boat, noticing as she did so that the barbed wire had now been fixed into place. Her mouth firmed. If Simeon's men had done their job properly yesterday, Lady wouldn't be lying in the veterinary hospital.

At the estate agent's her hopes disintegrated, and she was glad she had said nothing to George. The asking price was far too high—ridiculously high, in fact. She couldn't see anyone paying that sort of money.

Early that evening Andrew came to see her, his eyes worried behind his gold-rimmed glasses. 'I heard you were off sick. What's happened?' He looked with concern at her bandaged arm.

Candra grimaced. 'Lady got stuck in a roll of barbed wire. I tried to help her out. It's not as bad as it looks. But Lady had to have some stitches. She's still at the vet's.'

'Oh, dear,' he said. 'She will be all right?'

Candra nodded.

'I noticed the fencing.'

'Supposedly to keep vandals out,' commented Candra drily.

'Or because they've started work,' he said. 'I see there's a couple of diggers in there.'

Candra frowned quickly. 'Are you sure?'

Andrew nodded. 'I'm positive.'

'But he can't start work yet. His notice hasn't expired.'

'I don't imagine a little thing like that will stop him. He'll want to get most of the work done before the winter.'

Candra was furious. 'He said nothing to me this morning.'

'You saw him?'

'You bet I did. I went to tell him off about the barbed wire.'

'It seems to me that the sooner you move away from here, the better.'

Candra shook her head. 'There's no way I'm going to let Simeon Sterne intimidate me. He's probably had those diggers put there simply to frighten me.'

'You're fighting a losing battle, Candra.'

'Maybe I am,' she shrugged, 'but this is an issue that I really care about. Even though my grandfather no longer owns the land, I feel it affects me personally. I shan't back down.'

When Candra told Andrew about the cottage he said he knew one of the partners in the estate agent's. 'I'll have a word and see what he thinks the owner will come down to.'

'I'd be grateful,' said Candra.

'I'm not so sure about your living there, though. How about in the winter when you can't move your boat?'

'I'll have to walk to the main road and catch a bus. Or maybe the farm that's nearby will let me leave my car there. There are no insurmountable problems, Andrew. In fact, it should be quite fun.'

'Doesn't George have any family?'

'A married son who comes twice a week,' she told him. 'He's tried his hardest to persuade George to live with them, but he won't leave the canal. That's why the cottage would be ideal.'

When Candra picked up Lady the next morning she was shocked by the extent of her wounds. Her fur had been shaved where she was stitched, and there were more bald patches on her than hair. She came to Candra, wagging her tail, happy to see her, but she was subdued and nothing like her usual boisterous self. Candra felt like crying.

Instead of returning to the boat, she drove to her parents' home and asked her mother whether she would look after Lady. 'I can't leave her on her own,' she said. 'I'm frightened she might try to pull the stitches out.'

Mrs Drake was full of concern. 'Of course. Poor Lady, poor thing. Come on, girl, come along; we'll soon have you better.'

Candra smiled. Her mother was making more fuss of the dog than herself. 'I wish Uncle Jack hadn't sold that land to Simeon Sterne,' she said, 'then none of this would have happened. Couldn't you have persuaded him to carry out Gramps' wishes?'

Her mother shrugged. 'You know Jack. He never was interested in conservation. And your father says he can't understand why you're kicking up such a fuss. Stonely is no longer the sleepy little place it used to be, and it's not use pretending it is.'

In other words, she had not even tried to persuade her brother, Jack, to stipulate that the land was to be used as a nature reserve. Her husband had convinced her that building was inevitable. He was very good at inflicting his opinion on others. And the trouble was that everyone took notice of him. Candra had herself when she'd lived at home.

When Andrew came into her office later that afternoon, his news was not good. 'I'm sorry, Candra, someone's already made an offer on the cottage, not far off the original asking price.'

'I don't believe it,' gasped Candra. 'Who'd pay that sort of money?'

Andrew shrugged. 'Evidently someone was prepared to.'

Evidently. Candra was disappointed. She had lain in bed last night thinking about it. It would have been the perfect answer to their problem.

Every day, when she got home from work, Candra expected to find that Simeon Sterne's workmen had begun clearing the site, but every night it was exactly the same. She could not understand the reason for the earth-diggers.

And then, a week later, it began. She arrived home from the office to find *Four Seasons* covered in a layer of dust. George was sitting on his boat, pipe in mouth as usual, and he looked at her glumly.

'He can't do this,' said Candra sharply. 'Our time's not up. I shall go and see him tomorrow.'

But she had no need. Simeon Sterne came to see her. When he turned up, she had just showered and washed her hair. She felt the boat move as he stepped on to it, and then his gravelly voice called out to her through the hatchway.

'I'm here,' she said. 'Come on in. You're just the person I want to see.'

'I thought you might,' He wore casual beige trousers and a cream summer shirt, and Skye rushed straight to him and began licking his hand.

'What's the meaning of all this?' she demanded, waving her hand in the direction of the warehouse site.

'We're starting work.'

'So I see. And it doesn't matter that my boat gets covered in dust—inside as well, because I leave the windows open for Skye?'

He lifted his broad shoulders. 'I did warn you.'

'You gave me notice,' she snapped. 'It has not yet expired. You're breaking the law.' As she glared at him, Candra tried not to notice his sensual mouth.

'I don't think so,' he replied, smiling annoyingly. 'I would break the law if I tried to forcibly move you, but not to start work on my own land. It's a fine point, but not a moot one.'

'And you intend carrying on like this until I'm forced to leave because of the inconvenience?' Candra's eyes were a brilliant green, flashing her hostility, her whole stance that of a threatened wild animal.

'That is the general idea,' he admitted.

'Very clever, Mr Sterne,' she scorned, 'but you haven't taken my staying power into account. If I dig my heels in, nothing, and no one, moves me.'

'Interesting. May I sit down?'

'No, you may not,' she answered sharply. 'I have nothing further I wish to say to you.'

But he sat all the same. 'I really cannot understand why you're being so stubborn when you'll have to move in the end.'

Candra glared. 'Principle, Mr Sterne, but you wouldn't understand that.'

His mouth twisted wryly. 'You really do have a bad opinion of me, don't you?'

'Is it any wonder? You've done me no favours. All you've done is disrupt my life, and that of a dozen others as well.'

'None complained as loudly as you.'

'Because they didn't feel the same sense of injustice. I imagine my grandfather's turning in his grave.'

He shook his head and changed the subject. 'Have

you received the vet's bill?'

Candra pulled a sheet of paper out of her letter-rack and silently handed it to him.

He tucked it into his hip pocket without even looking. 'I'll see that it's paid.'

Candra had been tempted to pay the bill herself, but an inner voice told her that it was his fault, and why should she? And so it had sat there while she debated what to do. Lady still had to go back to have her stitches out and be given the all-clear. Barry would probably charge her for that as well.

'By the way, where's Lady?' Simeon asked.

'With my parents. She's very distressed. I couldn't leave her here alone.'

'And Skye, does he miss her?'

Candra nodded.

'How long will it be before she's better?'

'The wounds are healing, but it will be a few weeks before she's completely recovered.'

'I'd like to see her.'

She frowned. 'I don't think that's necessary.'

'No? As you say it's my fault, I really would like to see the extent of her injuries.'

'So that you can claim I was exaggerating?' she demanded crossly.

'Were you?'

'No, I was not.'

He laughed at her defensive stance. 'Why don't you sit down?'

'I'm waiting for you to go.'

'I thought I might spend the evening with you,' he said surprisingly. 'That is, if you've nothing else arranged?' He looked at her tousled wet hair and the cotton wrap she had pulled hurriedly on. 'Were you getting ready to go out?'

Reluctantly Candra shook her head.

'Good.'

'But I don't see what you're expecting to gain out of it,' she flashed. 'I shan't change my mind about moving.'

'The company of a beautiful lady for a few hours.'

Candra eyed him scornfully. 'I can't believe that you're short of female company.'

'No, I can't say I am,' he admitted, 'but none is as intriguing as you.'

Candra still felt there was some other motive for this visit. Nothing so simple as wanting to spend time with her. He wanted her out of his way, and he would use fair means or foul to do it. But curiosity got the better of her. 'I'll go and make myself decent,' she said reluctantly. 'There's whisky in that cupboard, or you can put on the kettle.'

'I'll have a Scotch,' he said, and his smile was brilliant, almost triumphant.

Candra instantly wished she had never agreed. She reached out a glass and the bottle and pushed them at him. 'I won't be long.'

'Take as long as you like,' he smiled, opening the bottle and pouring himself a generous measure. He looked as though he was prepared to settle down for the whole evening.

In her bedroom, Candra closed the folding door, wishing there were a bolt on it. She pulled on a yellow linen skirt and a cream silk-knit top with a scooped neck and short sleeves. She tugged a comb through her hair, but did not bother with make-up. She had no wish to impress Simeon Sterne.

When she returned to the central cabin, he was flicking through the pages of a magazine, Skye was curled up at his feet, and he looked totally relaxed.

There was a small settee on one side of the lounge and two wooden-armed easy chairs on the other. As he occupied most of the settee Candra chose one of the armchairs. She sat and looked at him, and he said, 'Aren't you going to join me?'

'I don't think so. I rarely drink, except when I'm entertaining.'

'And isn't that what you're doing now?' he asked with some amusement.

'Not voluntarily,' she replied sharply.

He took another sip of his drink, eyeing her steadily. 'It's a pity you're so much against me. I think you and I could be very good friends.'

'Is it?' she demanded. 'I think it's very natural, considering who you are.'

'The enemy,' he acknowledged gravely.

Candra found his presence filling the confined space. She had to sit with her feet tucked well in to avoid touching his outstretched legs. There wasn't room for him here, and she resented his inviting himself on board. His aftershave was faint but detectable, and she could not help but remember when she had been held against that hard, muscular body.

'How long have you had this boat?' he asked.

She dragged her eyes back to his face. 'Twelve months.'

'It's an odd choice.'

'I don't think so,' she defended. 'My grandfather, my paternal grandfather, that is, worked the boats, and his

father before him. My own father helped when he was
a boy. I know all about boats. I can handle one as well
as any man.'

His thick black brows rose. 'I'm impressed. I thought
you were one of those people who bought a boat because
it was the fashionable thing to do. I didn't realise it was
in your blood.'

'Well, now you know,' she shot back, 'and perhaps
you'll understand why I'm digging my heels in. It's not
only the development; I've wanted to live on a boat for
as long as I can remember.'

'There's no reason why you still can't.'

'But I want to live here, right here.'

His eyes glittered coldly. 'You're the most
unreasonable female I've ever met.'

'I don't think so, Mr Sterne. All I'm doing is sticking
up for myself.' For far too long she had let other people
walk all over her. But not any longer.

'That I understand,' he said, 'but not when the
outcome is inevitable. Tell me, what difference does it
make whether you move tomorrow or in a few weeks'
time?'

'It means,' she answered savagely, 'that I shall have
the satisfaction of knowing I've done all I can to stop
you.'

Not that her efforts would amount to anything, she
knew that. She had contacted her friends at the
Conservation Trust and they had said that it was too late.
If they had been notified earlier, et cetera, et cetera.

'Nothing or no one will stop me,' he told her firmly.

'But I can sure as hell make things difficult for you.'

'Or yourself,' he replied with an amused smile. 'Today
is only the beginning. The dust and dirt will not lessen.'

'You're enjoying this, aren't you?' she demanded angrily.

He lifted his powerful shoulders. 'It certainly breaks the monotony of life.'

How true that was. There hadn't been a dull moment since she'd heard the name Simeon Sterne. And she had to confess that he was exhilarating company; she hadn't felt so alive in a long time. His sexuality was such that it could not be ignored. She could feel her body responding of its own volition to the animal in him.

'Have you no inclination to get married?'

Candra's eyes shot wide at this sudden change of conversation. It was almost as though he had been following her own line of thought. 'None at all. I'm not a man-lover.'

'How about that guy who was here the other night? What does he mean to you?'

Candra's eyes flashed. 'He's nothing. My career is more important to me than marriage.'

'Ah, yes. You have ambition, I'd forgotten.'

'And you, of course, don't approve of women with ambition.' Candra's eyes once more flashed her scorn, and she stood up and moved to the other end of the boat, filling the kettle and lighting the stove.

To her annoyance he followed, leaning against the wall and watching as she reached out a cup and saucer and the jar of instant coffee. 'Do you want some?' she asked ungraciously as she put a spoonful into her cup.

'No, thank you. What makes you think I wouldn't approve?'

'Because it shows,' she answered coolly.

He frowned. 'In what way?'

'You disapprove of me, for one thing.'

'Have I ever said that?'

Candra lifted her shoulders. 'Not in so many words, but it's very clear.'

'Then maybe you should take a lesson in psychology, Candra. I do not disapprove of you, only your attitude.'

'What's the difference?' she demanded.

'I think that deep down inside, beyond that coldly defensive façade, there lurks a warm, passionate, caring woman.'

'Really?' she asked with a contemptuous toss of her head.

'I'm sure of it.'

'And you intend trying to break through my barriers and discover the true me?'

His lips quirked. 'It would be interesting.'

'It would be a waste of time,' she scorned. 'I'm not interested in any sort of relationship. But let us get one thing straight, Mr Sterne—the barrier between us is hatred. I detest the very sight of you.'

A muscle jerked in his jaw. 'Because of what I'm doing?'

'Because of the way you're harassing me.'

The muscle tensed again, his eyes narrowed until they were invisible, and he moved towards her.

Candra felt a quiver of unease. Had she goaded him too far? His hands came down on her shoulders, then slid up her neck, his thumbs on her throat. She froze with fear, her eyes wide, but she did not move. She kept her eyes on his and mentally dared him to hurt her.

CHAPTER FOUR

THE kiss was Candra's punishment. There was none of his earlier persuasiveness. She was held so hard against him that bone ground upon bone and her arms were pinned to her sides. She could not move or talk.

But somewhere through it Candra became aware of a dawning pleasure. Hardly discernible, a thin thread of excitement worming its way through her. And the thought, the very thought that this man, this hateful man, could do this to her, added furious strength to her struggles. She pitched and pulled and kicked and twisted, and finally broke free. 'You swine!' she spat, her eyes shooting savage sparks, her breast heaving as she fought for control.

He grinned. 'A wildcat as well.'

'And whose fault is it?'

His smile faded abruptly. 'A man can only take so much, Candra. Don't you know that?'

'And so can a woman,' she snapped.

Brows slid slowly upwards. 'Some man hurt you?'

Candra flung herself at the doors, swinging them wide with angry hands. 'My private life is no business of yours. Get out!'

'But I'm right, aren't I?' he insisted. 'It was a man who did this to you.'

'Did what?'

'Made you hate the whole male population. It's not simply because you don't agree with what I'm doing, it's because I'm a man. It's *me* you object to.'

'Don't flatter yourself,' she tossed smartly.

'But you also realise that you're fighting a losing battle—on both counts.'

'And what is that supposed to mean?' she frowned.

He smiled and ran the backs of his fingers gently down her cheek. 'This.'

Candra swallowed hard and resisted the temptation to knock his hand away, but she could not ignore the leaping of her pulses.

'Maybe it pleases you to deny feeling a response,' he went on, his narrowed blue eyes penetrating through her clothes to her heated skin beneath, 'but feel it you did, and who knows? Maybe I'll be the one to make you forget all about your ambition, and you'll become truly a woman.'

'Are you suggesting I'm not a woman now?' gasped Candra, unable to credit his audacity.

His smile was slow and cynical. 'You look like a woman, a very attractive one, you even feel and smell like a woman, but that's as far as it goes.'

'It doesn't mean to say I'm not capable,' retorted Candra, her humiliation cutting deep. 'I simply haven't time for that sort of a relationship.'

'There's always time for love, Candra.'

'Is there?' she demanded caustically. 'The way I see things, men are only happy when they're ordering their womenfolk around. And I've had enough of that. I'm my own boss now, and I intend to stay that way.'

'Would you care to tell me about it?'

'Why?'

'Because it might help me to understand you better.'

'And you might change your mind about letting me stay?'

His eyes narrowed. 'You know there's no chance of that.'

'Then there's no chance I'll tell you about my private life.'

'We're not all the same, you know. Most men prefer to love and cherish their women.'

'You're speaking from experience, of course,' she scorned.

A shadow crossed his face, then was gone. 'It's a fact of life.'

She did not believe him; she never would. He had done nothing but try to order her around since they had met. Perhaps she would tell him. It might make him see exactly why she was so much against him and men in general.

'You're very much like my father, do you know that?' Her grey eyes were fixed firmly on his face. 'He tried to rule my life. And in those days I hadn't the guts to stand up for myself. That's why I'm working in an office now, instead of with animals. It was what *he* wanted. Everything I did was what *he* wanted. My brother was the same. I used to let him order me around without a word of complaint. But not any more.'

'Maybe you shouldn't be condemning them, but thanking them for making you the strong character you are now?'

'It was not only them,' she flashed. 'I had a boyfriend who also tried to take over my life. He was an only child and used to getting his own way. I was always expected to change my plans to fall in with his. There were no compromises.' And to begin with she'd been too madly in love to care.

'But gradually I began to realise how selfish he was.

And the next time he asked me to drop everything and go with him, I refused. I told him I'd had enough of being his slave, and wasn't going to let my friends down again just because of him. He was so angry, it was unbelievable.'

'And did you see him again?' Simeon had listened patiently while she talked, no expression at all on his face.

'No.' She swallowed hard. 'He had a fatal accident that very same day. Naturally I blamed myself, and I was very upset, but I swore I'd let no other man rule my life. And I mean it. So now I've told you, you can get out.'

'If you absolutely insist.'

'I do.'

'Then goodnight, Candra.' Before she could stop him he had taken her face between his palms and pressed a kiss to her brow. 'Goodnight, my fiery friend, and thank you for explaining why you're so much against me. But I think you're wrong. As I said before, we're not all the same.'

He was gone before she could answer. The boat rocked as he stepped off, and Candra watched through the window until he was out of sight. Not all the same indeed. Maybe Andrew wasn't; he would never hurt her. But most men were, and Simeon in particular. She wanted nothing to do with him.

With each day that passed the dust on her boat got thicker. There seemed no point in washing it off when it would be just as bad tomorrow.

Lady's wounds were almost healed, and Candra fetched her home. She and Skye raced up and down the canal bank in their happiness at being together.

But Candra's days here were limited, and at the beginning of the final week, when she would either have to move or be moved, George Miller greeted her when she got home from work with the broadest smile she had ever seen.

'You look happy, George. What's happened? Have you found somewhere to live?'

He nodded. 'I'm renting the old lock cottage. My son found out about it. I'm moving in tomorrow.'

Candra was surprised, but pleased. 'I knew it had been sold recently, but I didn't realise it was going to be rented out. It's marvellous news. It calls for a celebration.'

She fetched a bottle of wine and they sat on his foredeck sipping it. 'What do you think,' she asked after a while, 'about my tying up by the cottage? It will be company for you, and help me out of a sticky situation.'

'Don't see no problem,' said George.

But the next morning, when George's son came early to help him move, he shook his head. 'I'm sorry, it's not possible—the Water Board won't allow it. The canal's too narrow there. They say it would restrict access to the lock. My father's even having to sell this boat. There's a little punt available for shopping trips, but I doubt he'll use it. Diane will see that he's never short of anything.'

And so Candra's last hope was dashed.

Sunday midnight was her deadline. She had seen nothing more of Simeon since their evening together, but she was not surprised to see him striding towards her late in the afternoon.

Candra knew it was a foolish game she was playing,

but it had turned into a battle of nerves, and she intended
staying right up until midnight, as she had vowed she
would. Then she would move down the canal and tie up
on the towpath side for a day or two.

It really did look as though she would have to move
right away from Stonely, and, although it didn't present
a real problem, Candra resented being forced into this
situation. Therefore, when Simeon stepped on to her
boat and his bowed head appeared in the doorway, she
was less than welcoming.

Instead of inviting him inside, she climbed up the
steps and stood on the stern, her chin high, one hand
resting on the tiller, the other on her hip. She said
nothing, she simply waited for him to state the reason
for his visit.

'You have seven more hours, Candra. Are you
planning to move in the dark?'

The icy blue hardness of his eyes had never been so
unnerving. 'I'll move when I'm ready,' she said tightly.

'Even George has gone.'

Candra's eyes flashed. 'I think it stinks, making an
old man like him move at his time of life.'

'I believe he has found somewhere satisfactory.'

'With no thanks to you,' she snapped.

He ignored her anger. 'I take it you've made
arrangements?'

'Actually, no.'

'This is ridiculous.'

She heard the swift angry intake of breath, and
wished he weren't standing quite so close. It was
impossible in a situation like this to ignore his virility.
It had been bothering her for days—ever since that
punishing kiss, in fact. 'I'm merely making a point, Mr

Sterne.'

'At eight o'clock in the morning that wall is being demolished. Excavation is already finished on the other side. We're ready to start digging away the opening to the marina.'

Her eyes widened.

'So I would suggest you move now.' His jaw was tense, a muscle jerking spasmodically, and he looked as though he was prepared to start the boat and move it himself.

Candra shrugged, pretending unconcern. 'In that case I have no choice. A pity you didn't tell me earlier that you were so far advanced.'

'You mean it would have made a difference?' The sceptical tone of his voice told her that he did not believe it for one second.

'I wouldn't have left it quite so late.'

'So where are you going now?'

She spread her hands airily. 'I shall tie up somewhere the other side of the lock. I imagine I'll have to move about a bit until I can find permanent moorings. It won't be so easy getting to the office, but I'll survive.'

'There's still my friend's place.'

And Candra knew she had no choice. 'Where does he live?'

'I'll come and show you.'

That was the last thing Candra wanted. This man was irritating her beyond measure. 'Just tell me.'

But he was adamant. 'It's best if I take you.'

'How far away is it?' she demanded hostilely.

'About a mile.'

Candra was so uptight that she could willingly have shoved him into the canal. Hadn't her confession the other day meant anything to him? Didn't he realise this was the very sort of situation she had tried to avoid? She did not want to be manoeuvred like a piece on a chessboard.

'I'll untie you,' he said.

She started the engine and waited for Simeon to step back on board, tempted to go without him, but there was no point when she did not know where she was going. He coiled the ropes carefully, then stood on the stern deck with her and the dogs, and Candra was conscious of him watching her every move.

Soon they were travelling through beautiful open countryside, and it was hard to imagine that they were so close to the town. This was what Candra liked best about canals—they provided a whole new vista, an entirely different dimension to the landscape.

'You handle her well,' he said, after they had been going for ten minutes.

A compliment indeed! Candra shot him a quick glance. 'I told you, I was taught at an early age.'

'Ah yes, I remember you saying you started when you were just out of nappies. That I would have liked to see.'

Candra flashed him an angry glance. 'OK, so I was exaggerating. But you shouldn't have spoken to me as though I were an idiot.'

'I didn't know you then.'

'And you think you do now?'

'Probably not everything, but there's time.'

She looked at him sharply. 'I doubt it. I don't like what you've done to me. I don't like accepting your help now, and I don't plan to see you again.'

'That might be unavoidable.'

'Why?' frowned Candra swiftly.

'Because——' He stopped abruptly as they came round a bend in the canal, and pointed in front of them. 'There's the house. Stop by those trees.' Then he went on, 'Because—I happen to be living in my friend's house for the time being.'

Candra drew in a swift, disbelieving breath, her head jerking. 'What is this, some kind of joke?' All sorts of hideous thoughts raced through her mind.

'No joke, Candra, it's the truth. My friend is overseas at the moment, and he gave me free use of his house while my own is being renovated.'

She frowned, a deep frown that gouged her brow. 'So he doesn't know about me? I can just imagine what he'll say when he comes back and finds a boat tied at the bottom of his garden.'

'Rick won't mind. He's hardly ever at home.'

'But I mind,' she thrust angrily. 'You've deceived me. You must know I'd never have come if I'd known you were going to be here.'

'Oh, yes,' he said with a faint smile. 'I realised that. But I had to move you today one way or another.'

Candra swallowed the bitter taste in her mouth and concentrated on bringing *Four Seasons* smoothly in to the side, where there was a purpose-built paved mooring area. Much as she hated to admit it, this was an idyllic spot. She had seen this house frequently on her travels up and down the canal, and had always envied whoever owned it.

The line of dark green cypress trees hid the boat from the main building, and, although the lawns ran down to the water's edge, and there were paths cutting through them up to the house, she would not need to use them to reach the lane that ran alongside the property. She could follow the curve of the canal and climb up at the side of the bridge. That way she would avoid Simeon altogether.

Her spirits, which had fallen drastically when she'd discovered he was living here, lifted. Her only problem would be the dogs. They would not be able to have the freedom they'd had before.

As if reading her mind, Simeon said, 'What are your dogs like where gardens are concerned? Do they dig up rose-beds and the like?'

'Of course not,' replied Candra indignantly. 'They're far too well trained.'

'In which case,' he said, 'I see no reason why they should not be left free to roam the grounds. My friend has a full-time gardener who'll keep his eye on them, but, in any case, they can't get out unless they swim the canal. They'll make good guard dogs for the house as well as your boat.'

'I'm having my doubts about that,' snapped Candra. 'They let you on my boat.' No one had ever before been able to win their confidence so easily.

He grinned. 'I once had a German Shepherd myself. I know how to handle them. I don't think they'd easily admit anyone else.'

Truthfully, neither did Candra.

Simeon jumped off the boat and grabbed the ropes, expertly tying *Four Seasons* to the rings that were cemented into the ground. It was not the first time he had done this sort of thing, that was for sure, thought Candra. 'Doesn't your friend have a boat?' she called as she cut the engine.

'He hasn't time for one,' came the negative reply,

'though I believe the people who owned the house before did. There's water and electricity. You should have no trouble getting the necessary permission to stay here permanently. It's a perfect spot, don't you think? I'm tempted to make my friend an offer for this place. I like it here. It's much nicer than my town house.'

Candra groaned inwardly. If he did buy this house, then she would have to move again. There was no way she wanted to live so close to him permanently. The dogs were exploring the garden, the boat was tied up, and there was nothing else left for him to do. So why didn't he go? 'Thank you for bringing me here,' she said primly.

He nodded. 'I'll leave you to settle in. Come up to the house afterwards for a drink.'

'Thank you, but no, thank you,' she retorted. 'You should know that I have no wish to develop any sort of a relationship.'

He frowned at her sharp words. 'I was merely being neighbourly. If you wish to keep yourself to yourself, then so be it.' With a curt nod, he turned and made his way up to the house.

Candra felt embarrassed, but what else was she supposed to think? Or did he go around kissing girls all the time, expecting them to read nothing into it? Not that she wanted anything to do with him, she hastened to assure herself, but he was an extremely attractive man, and the first one to stir her blood since she'd put the shutters up after Craig died.

She made herself a sandwich and a cup of tea, and tried to dismiss him from her thoughts. Lady returned, but there was no sign of Skye. She whistled and called, and in the end went looking for him.

The grounds to the house, about three acres in all, were beautiful. Closely shaved lawns with conifer and heather beds, a rockery and a pool filled with Japanese Koi, covered with a net to keep away the herons. A fountain, a swimming-pool and a red cedarwood building next to it, which she presumed housed a sauna. A summer-house high up on the hill, greenhouses. It was absolute perfection.

On the terrace which overlooked both the swimming-pool and the canal were tubs and hanging baskets of bright red geraniums, purple and white petunias and clouds of blue lobelia. Sliding glass doors stood slightly open—and inside was Skye!

Candra marched up to the doors angrily and called to him. Simeon Sterne looked unsmilingly back, and Skye made no move.

'Here, boy.' The dog normally obeyed her every command, but now he looked at Simeon and wagged his tail.

'At least he's prepared to be friends,' said Simeon coolly. It's a pity you don't follow his example.'

Candra fumed and slid the door open wider. 'You know that's impossible. I have no wish to be friends with you, Mr Sterne, ever. Skye, heel!' she commanded firmly.

Immediately the Alsatian came to her and sat down. 'You're teaching my dog to be disobedient,' she crisped. 'Please don't do it again.' Then she turned on her heel and began to walk away.

'Candra, wait!' He pushed himself up and came across the room towards her. But whatever it was he was going to say Candra never found out, because at that moment a girl walked round the side of the house towards them.

Candra did not think she had ever seen anyone quite so beautiful. She had raven-black hair cut dramatically short, and a golden tan. She was wearing a red body-hugging dress with matching lipstick, nail polish and high-heeled shoes. She was probably aged about twenty-six, and had eyes for no one but Simeon.

'Simeon, darling, I've been ringing the front doorbell like mad. I thought you must be away.'

He smiled warmly when he saw the girl, his whole face and attitude changing. 'It's out of order, Briony. Why didn't you let me know you were coming?'

'I wanted to surprise you.'

He held out his arms and she went into them, and Candra turned away. The expression on his face said it all.

Surprisingly, he called her back. 'Candra, don't go. You must meet Briony—a very close friend of mine, Briony Hall.' And to Briony, 'This is my new neighbour, Candra Drake.'

'Neighbour?' frowned Briony. 'I don't understand.'

'Candra lives on a narrow-boat,' he explained with yet another warm smile. 'And as she was—er—forced to move, I invited her to bring her boat here.'

That was one way of putting it, thought Candra bitterly. 'Don't worry, I was just leaving,' she told the other girl. 'I'm not encroaching on your property, you can have Simeon all to yourself. I simply came to fetch my dog, who was making a bit of a nuisance of himself. Goodbye, Simeon.'

'I'll see you in the morning,' he said, with a sudden angry frown.

'You will?' she asked.

'I presume you do need a lift into Stonely?'

'Oh, yes, of course.' She smiled with a cheerfulness she was far from feeling. 'Thank you very much. I'll pick my own car up at lunchtime, then you won't have to bother about me again. I'm sorry I'm such a nuisance.'

Candra whirled away, but before she had taken more than a few steps she was conscious that the two of them had disappeared inside the house, and it surprised her that she felt hurt by Simeon's obvious interest in Briony.

She wondered how long they had known each other, and exactly what the situation was between them. Was she someone special, or merely one of many girlfriends? Candra was glad she had refused to join him for a drink. It would have been far more difficult to extricate herself had she been sitting comfortably in his lounge when Briony arrived.

It was a relief that from her boat she could not see the house, though her imagination worked overtime. She could picture them together sipping drinks, Briony cuddled up close to him, too close, her body pressed against his, their hearts beating as one. Candra knew the feeling. It had happened to her against her will, so what would it be like if she held nothing back?

As it was a warm evening she sat out on the deck of her boat, her head resting back against the cabin, her eyes closed. All she could hear were the sounds of the countryside, the plaintive bleat of a lamb, a cow's insistent mooing, droning insects, the occasional plop of a fish as it jumped out of the water. And then voices.

She opened her eyes and sat upright, and there were Briony and Simeon standing at the water's edge. His arm was about her shoulders, hers was around his waist, and they were seemingly oblivious to her presence, though Candra guessed he had brought the girl down here deliberately. The dogs ran across to them, but Candra got up and went inside. She had no wish to be a spectator.

When Skye and Lady came back she presumed they had gone, and when a few minutes later she heard a car start up she knew Briony had left the house. But alone, or with Simeon? She told herself she did not care, that she was glad about Briony because it meant he would leave her alone. And that was what she wanted. Wasn't it?

At ten o'clock Candra got ready for bed. She thought she saw a glimmer of light up at the house, but couldn't be sure. Simeon was very much in her thoughts when she fell asleep, and again when she awoke, much to her disgust. What was wrong with her, that she was letting this man bother her so much?

She pulled on a tracksuit and took the dogs for a long walk through some woods on the other side of the lane. Then she filled the kettle and made toast, but when she turned on the shower afterwards there was no water. Not a dribble. She knew immediately what was wrong. Her water tank was empty. She had been meaning to fill it up all week.

To add to her troubles, she had no hose. The old rubber one that had been on the boat when she bought it was perished, and she had thrown it away. There had been a communal one at the site, so she had never felt the need to buy another. And now she had no means of filling her water tank!

Metaphorically shrugging, Candra fetched her kettle and filled it from the outside tap. She would forgo her shower and have a good wash instead. But as she stepped back on to *Four Seasons* Simeon came striding towards her. His black hair was damp and slightly wavy. He wore the inevitable white shirt, open at the collar, and the trousers to a navy pin-striped suit. 'Is something wrong?'

'I've no water for a shower,' she admitted reluctantly, unable to stop her heart clamouring at the sight of his savage maleness. 'And no hose to fill the tank. '

His brows rose reprovingly. 'Tut, tut. I had you written down as a very organised person.'

Candra shrugged, his mockery rankling. 'No one's infallible. But it doesn't matter. I'll buy a hose today and fill up tonight.'

'I expect there's one around here somewhere,' he said. 'But I suggest you come up to the house for your shower.'

Candra's grey eyes widened. 'I can't do that.'

'Why not? Are you afraid?'

'Of course not,' she said quickly.

A brow lifted as though he did not believe her. 'Then what's your excuse?'

Candra shrugged. 'I suppose I don't have one, except propriety.'

'Who's to know,' he asked sardonically, 'unless you tell them? Don't worry about soap and towels. You'll find everything you need.'

She swallowed the last of her misgivings and followed him. The house was as beautiful inside as out. Elegant was the word that came to mind, and the bathroom he showed her to on the ground floor was simply stunning. She stood for a moment, wide-mouthed.

A curved grey marble platform held a sunken bath and a shower cubicle—and a porcelain leopard! The rest of the floor was carpeted in grey, and the tiles on the walls were finely striped in black and red. There were mirrored wall cupboards above the black and gold washbasins, reflecting light from an opposite window. Candra had never seen a bathroom like it.

But there was no time to waste. She quickly stripped off and stood beneath the fierce shower jets. It was an invigorating shower, nothing like the gentle, sometimes cantankerous one on the boat. She was thoroughly enjoying it when Simeon banged on the door and told her to hurry.

Immediately she turned off the water, opened the screen door, and stepped out. As she did so, her foot slipped on the marble floor, her arms flailed the air, and she landed on her back with a thud that jarred every bone in her body.

The lock on the door did not work—that was one thing she had noticed when she went in—and Simeon, hearing her cry, came running into the room. Candra did not know which worried her most, the pain, or Simeon's seeing her naked.

'I slipped,' she said unnecessarily.

'Can you get up?'

'I think so.'

He held out his arm and she clung to him heavily, then he picked up one of the black and gold towels and wrapped it around her. But not before his eyes had taken in every inch of her body. It was a long, slow appraisal, from the very tips of her pink-painted toenails right up to the tousled wetness of her hair, and it set every nerve-end tingling.

Candra scowled her anger. She did not want anything like this to happen. She was finished with men, especially of his breed, and he knew it.

'Are you sure you're all right?' he frowned, noting her changing emotions.

Candra nodded and managed a wry smile. 'No bones broken, although I'll probably be black and blue by this evening.'

'I have some liniment, if you'd like me to——'

'No, thanks,' she cut in at once, alarmed at the thought of his hands on her body.

His mouth tightened. 'I was not suggesting I rub it in, merely that I fetch it. Why do you persist in misconstruing everything I say?'

'That's what I meant, as well,' said Candra, her chin lifting haughtily. She looked him in the eye and dared him to call her a liar.

He frowned, but said nothing, watching as she crossed the bathroom to the stool on which her clothes were neatly folded. A pain shot through her back with each step that she took, and it was impossible to hide her agony.

'I think I should call a doctor,' rasped Simeon.

'Don't be ridiculous,' she snapped. 'I'll be fine in a minute.'

'The last thing I want on my hands is a martyr,' he returned crisply.

'I prefer to call it bravery.' Her tone was caustic. 'And, if you wouldn't mind leaving the room, I'll get dressed. I don't want to be late for work.'

'You're surely not still thinking of going?'

'But of course. A few bruises won't stop me.'

'You're crazy,' he said.

'I have an important meeting to attend.'

'And work comes before anything else? I should have known. Candra Drake, the dedicated career woman. Nothing will stop her on her climb up the ladder to success.'

His mockery incensed her, but she kept her voice level. 'Please get out of here.'

'If you insist, but I would suggest I fetch your office clothes from the boat. It's ridiculous getting dressed twice when it's not necessary.'

Candra fought an inner battle with herself and lost. 'Very well. There's a grey suit in my wardrobe, and a red and white blouse. I'd like my red shoes as well, please, and my bag's on the bed.'

He nodded.

'The boat keys are on a hook by the door.'

She spent the next five minutes wishing she hadn't let him go. The thought of him going through her wardrobe gave rise to all sorts of strange feelings, and when he finally returned with clean undies as well colour flamed her cheeks.

She dressed as hurriedly as she could, and they met the gardener on their way out. He was introduced to the dogs and they sniffed him and approved, and Candra felt happy about leaving them free.

But when she sat beside Simeon in his car she could not help remembering that his hands had been on the clothes that she wore, the very intimate clothes that she wore next to her skin. And with the thought came the discovery that he was beginning to get through to her. And she did not want that to happen. She did not want to fall in love. She did not want a man in her life, especially someone as dictatorial as Simeon.

CHAPTER FIVE

SIMEON turned to Candra as he pulled up outside Thorag Pharmaceuticals. 'If you don't feel up to driving home tonight, give me a ring and I'll fetch you.'

'It won't be necessary,' she answered sharply, 'I can tell you that now. It's nice to know you'll be at the house if I need you, but other than that I think we should keep our distance. Goodbye, Mr Sterne.' And she climbed out of the car before he could answer.

Candra felt stiff and sore all day long, but it was nothing she could not cope with, and she had no intention of asking Simeon to drive her home. She discovered that her water tank had been filled and there was a hose for future use, but several days went by without her seeing Simeon again, which surprised her, considering his concern when she had fallen.

Then the gardener told her that he had been called away on business. 'He phoned Pauline and told her. I'm sorry, I thought you knew.'

'Pauline?' Another girlfriend?

'My wife. She does a spot of cleaning at the house. She's very fond of Simeon, even does his laundry for him.'

By the end of the week Simeon had still not returned. The weather, which had been fairly mixed, turned hot and sunny, and after lunch Candra put on her bikini and lay on the little bit of grass near the boat. Other narrow-boats came past, their occupants calling out a cheerful greeting, commenting on the good weather, hoping it would last.

The dogs lay panting at her side. It really was hot, one of the best days they'd had this year, and Candra thought longingly of the swimming-pool. Pauline and Geoffrey weren't here today; she had the whole place to herself. Why not? Up until now she had kept to her own corner of the garden, but surely Simeon wouldn't mind?

She fetched a towel from the boat and ran across, diving cleanly into the water. It was bliss, sheer bliss. Cold at first, but she soon got used to it. After several energetic laps, she lay on her back and floated, looking up at the clear blue sky. She closed her eyes and felt the warmth of the sun on her face and heard the faint drone of insects, then the sudden roar of Simeon's voice, 'What the hell do you think you're doing?'

Candra twisted herself upright and faced him. 'What does it look like?'

'I don't remember giving you permission.'

She was amazed at the coldness in his tone. 'I didn't think you'd mind.'

'Well, I damn well do mind.'

Unable to understand why he was so angry, Candra waded to the side and pulled herself out. 'Surely I'm doing no harm? You look as though you ought to be relaxing yourself.' His face was taut with tiredness.

'Which I would do if you weren't here,' he snarled.

Candra eyed him hostilely. 'Are you forgetting that you're the one who suggested I move here?'

'I didn't expect you to make free use of the facilities.'

'What's the matter?' she demanded. 'Have you had a bad week and decided to take it out on me?'

'That among other things,' he grated, 'but I have no intention of explaining myself.' His eyes, on her face, were as hard and expressionless as marbles.

Candra picked up her towel and wrapped it around her. The dogs, who had begun barking excitedly when he shouted, had quietened. 'It's easy to see why you've never married,' she said coldly. 'No woman would ever put up with such unreasonable behaviour.'

It was the wrong thing to say. If he had looked angry before, he was positively livid now. His face flushed an ugly red, his eyes narrowed, and Candra stepped back a pace. 'I was married once, Candra.' His tone was so quiet that it was frightening.

But she went on regardless, 'And what happened—did she divorce you?'

His eyes flicked her raw. 'Marie died—five years ago today.'

Candra clapped her hands to her mouth. 'Oh, I'm sorry. I didn't realise. Oh, dear, I really am sorry. I'd never have said that if I'd . . .' What words could she use to express her regret? She really had put her foot in it this time.

'I'm over it now,' he said bitterly.

'There were no children?' she dared to ask.

Several taut seconds went by before he answered. 'My wife was pregnant when she died.'

Candra closed her eyes. This was awful, far worse than when Craig had died. How she wished she had kept her mouth shut. 'I'm sorry,' she said, and how inadequate it sounded. 'I shouldn't have said what I did, it was uncalled for. Please forgive me.' Unhappily she walked away, and Skye and Lady followed sedately. They always sensed her moods and adjusted their own to match.

She lay down again in the sun behind the cypress

trees, and a short time later she heard Simeon dive into the pool. The dogs raced across the garden to see what was going on, and Candra half expected to hear him shout at them to go away, but all was quiet except for the splash of water as he swam up and down. He swam for a long time, as though punishing himself, and when eventually all was silent she wondered whether he was lying in the sun or whether he'd gone back indoors. The dogs didn't return, so she guessed he might still be outside—and they were keeping him company. Traitors!

Finally Candra decided she'd had enough sun for one day. With a bit of luck it would be out again tomorrow. There would be no swim in the pool, though, that was for sure. It was a pity; she'd really enjoyed it.

When Candra awoke on Sunday morning it was, as she had hoped, another glorious day, and she opened the doors and pushed back the slide to let the early morning sun into the boat. The dogs raced out, but the first thing she saw was Simeon standing on the canal-side a few yards away, gazing abstractedly into the water. 'Good morning,' she ventured, wondering what sort of a reception she would get. She still felt uncomfortable about her gaffe.

'Good morning, Candra.' He spoke cheerfully, as though yesterday had never happened. But when he began walking towards her she remembered she was still wearing her nightdress—what there was of it! Short, sheer and impractical, but ideal for hot summer nights.

'What a sight for sore eyes,' he said. 'If it's a deliberate attempt to raise my temperature, you're succeeding.'

As his eyes flickered over her, Candra felt acutely conscious of her nakedness beneath the fine silk. And as her body responded to his appraisal, her breasts hardened, her nipples pushing through the soft material.

He missed nothing. 'I'll run the dogs while you get dressed,' he said at length. 'Not that I don't prefer you like that, but I am human—and there's only so much a man can take.'

Since he had forgotten his bad mood of yesterday, Candra decided it would be churlish to refuse, so she smiled and nodded. 'Thank you, I'd appreciate it.'

One good turn deserves another, she told herself after he had walked away, so, after showering and pulling on a green and white sundress, she grilled bacon and fried eggs and when he came back breakfast was ready.

'I hope you haven't already eaten?' she asked anxiously, hoping her good deed wasn't going to backfire.

Simeon shook his head. 'But I rarely have breakfast. You shouldn't have gone to this trouble.'

Candra shrugged. 'I had to cook my own.' Though, if she were truthful, she never ate breakfast either. Perhaps a slice of toast, but nothing cooked.

They sat facing each other at her table in the dining area and Candra hoped she hadn't made a mistake. She did not want him to think that she was weakening, that this was a sign of things to come.

'Do you go away on business often?' she asked, feeling a need to break the silence that had settled between them. His presence was compelling and overpowering. The air felt suffocatingly thick, and her heart beat twice as fast as normal. 'I wondered what had happened when I didn't see you for several days.'

His black brows rose. 'You missed me? How surprising. It was your suggestion that we didn't get too—*familiar*.' He put deliberate emphasis on the word. 'I though you'd prefer it.'

Candra frowned. 'You're surely not suggesting that you went away because of me?'

'I'd like to say yes,' he said, 'but actually it was purely business.' He fed the last piece of egg into his mouth and put down his knife and fork. 'A word of advice, Candra. Don't cut yourself off altogether because of what happened in your past. There's more to life than carving a place for yourself in the world of business.'

'Not for me there isn't,' she said firmly.

'You're still putting me in the same category?'

'What choice have I?' she demanded. 'You made me move my boat against my will, you brought me here against my will, and you want us to be friends—against my will.'

'I didn't ask you to invite me to breakfast.'

'I didn't ask you to walk my dogs.'

Anger deepened his frown. He picked up his teacup, cradling it in his big strong hands, watching her over the brim as he took a sip. The whites of his eyes were clear and bright, and there were tiny specks of gold in the blue that Candra had never noticed before. They were beautiful eyes, mirroring his chameleon moods. 'Dammit, Candra, this is ridiculous. Are you saying that you prefer that wimp you were with the other week?'

'Andrew's a good friend,' she protested. 'And I don't know why it bothers you when you've got Briony hanging around your neck.'

His lips unexpectedly quirked. 'Do I detect a note of jealousy?'

'Jealousy is the last emotion I'd feel where your girlfriends are concerned,' she spat.

'That's good,' he said with a triumphant smile, 'because I've asked her round for a swim this afternoon. I'd like you to join us.'

The gall of the man. After ordering her out of the pool yesterday, he was now inviting her to use it. Her chin lifted and her eyes flashed. 'No, thank you.'

He laughed at her aggression and slid out of his seat. 'It was a fine breakfast, thank you. And I'm sure you'll change you mind, if only to satisfy your curiosity about Briony.'

'I doubt it,' she called after him as he left the boat. If his invitation had been for her alone, she might have accepted. Not because she wanted to be friends, nothing of the kind—it was a perfect day for swimming, that was all.

Candra washed up and tidied the boat, preparing a few vegetables in readiness for lunch, ironing the blouse and skirt she had washed yesterday, then, with nothing more to do, she sat outside in the sun.

As one hour stretched into two she realised that Simeon was right. It would be crucifyingly lonely here if she denied herself his company altogether. But she certainly had no intention of making a threesome with him and Briony.

She cooked her lunch, but didn't eat it. She changed into her bikini and stretched out in the sun. When a shadow fell across her she opened her eyes and Simeon stood watching her.

'I've not changed my mind,' she told him at once,

pushing herself up on her elbows. He wore brief white swimming-trunks which accentuated the teak-brown of his skin. He was powerfully muscled and looked even taller.

'That's a pity—because I've just had a call from Briony to say she can't make it.'

And he thought he would make do with her instead! 'I can't believe your conceit,' she spat.

He grinned. 'It seemed to me like an ideal opportunity for us to really get to know one another.'

'I don't know why you're so persistent.' She frowned. But how tempting the thought of that cool silky water was!

'Believe me, I can be very persistent.' He held out his hand and he did not move until she finally, hesitantly, allowed him to pull her up.

Nor did he let her go as they walked to the pool and Candra felt an intense but unwanted awareness. A pair of loungers sat in readiness, towels, umbrellas. Were they for her, or Briony? At the thought Candra twisted out of his grasp and ran for the pool, diving cleanly into the blue sparkling water.

Simeon followed, and when she surfaced he was beside her and his gaze was frankly admiring. 'You're a strong swimmer.'

'With us spending so much time on boats, my father insisted I learn at an early age.' The way he had insisted she do most things in her life. 'I swam for my school and college, and almost made it to the Olympics,' she added proudly.

'Is that so? Then how about a race? Say ten lengths. The loser buys dinner on Friday night at Hey House.'

Candra eyed him warily. Either way it meant she

would have to go out with him, but it might be fun pitting her strength against his. They'd had more than one battle of wills. This was something else. She could put up with his company for an hour or two if it meant getting the better of him now. She laughed and nodded. 'You're on.'

She felt suddenly charged with excitement, and her eyes sparkled into his as he began the countdown.

'One—two—three, *go*!'

Before she had completed one length, Candra knew she had a battle on her hands. Against an average male swimmer she could win easily, but Simeon was undoubtedly above average.

For the first four lengths they were neck and neck, then gradually he inched ahead. Candra decided to reserve some of her energy, let him think he was winning, let him push himself to his limit, then she would surge ahead and win.

But by the seventh length she knew she had left it too late. He was now almost a whole length ahead, grinning every time they met. She surged forward, bringing in new reserves of energy, surprising Simeon, and at the end of the race was only a few yards behind him.

'My congratulations,' he said. 'You're better than I thought.'

Candra was not quite sure whether he was mocking or admiring her, and she looked at him warily.

'Nevertheless,' he went on, 'you lost—which means you buy the dinner.' There was a note of satisfaction in his voice.

'I wouldn't count on winning another time, if I were you,' Candra retorted. 'Not now I know what I'm up against.'

'Fighting talk, eh?' and this time there was definite mockery in this tone.

'I think I could just about manage it.'

There was a light of challenge in her eyes, and he laughed, a deep, throaty laugh that chased the lines from his face and made him look years younger. 'You're on, Candra. Let's make it a week from today.' He hauled himself out of the pool then turned to help her. He didn't let her go when they were standing. Instead his arms slid behind her back, and she was pulled against the long, hard, cool, length of him.

Candra's body raced with an excitement she had never felt with Craig, and certainly not with Andrew. For once she did not want to resist him. She wanted his kisses. She wanted his hands on her body; she wanted to feel his strength and his maleness. It was insanity, but she did.

The day had worked its magic. The hot summer sun and the caressing water, and a Simeon who wasn't for once her enemy. Her eyes shone up into his and his mouth came down on hers. Desire sped through her limbs, and mindlessly she pressed herself closer. Tomorrow could take care of itself.

'Simeon. Where are you?'

Their moment of intimacy was rudely shattered.

'Simeon, it's me, Briony. I——' The girl came to an abrupt, shocked halt.

Candra pulled away, embarrassed, but Simeon looked totally unconcerned.

'I found I could come after all,' the dark girl finished lamely, her wide violet eyes shooting daggers at Candra.

'A couple of minutes earlier and you could have joined us,' smiled Simeon. 'We've just had a race, and

would you believe that Candra almost won? She's a
very fine swimmer.'

'And was the kiss her reward?' It was a light-hearted
question, but Candra sensed the venom beneath and,
turning away, she dived back into the water.

She swam a couple of lengths before daring to glance
in their direction. Briony had discarded her clothes and
wore the briefest of black bikinis, and Simeon was
rubbing oil into her back. Candra felt an unexpected stab
of jealousy, and wished with all her heart that she had
never accepted his invitation.

Climbing swiftly out of the pool, she raced back to
her boat. She heard Simeon call her name, but ignored
him. Her towel was still spread out on the grass and she
flung herself down, her fingers curled into fists, every
pulse jumping in anger. Skye and Lady came and lay at
her side.

For the first time her self-discipline had cracked, and
she'd felt a stirring of interest in a man. What a fool,
when he was clearly more interested in Briony. It was
evident now that he had simply been amusing himself
at her expense. But never again!

The more she thought about the situation, the madder
she got, and in the end she jumped up and took a long,
cool shower. But it did nothing to ease her anger. She
pulled on a shirt and jeans, and did not venture out again
until it was time to run the dogs.

There was a red MG in the drive, which suggested
Briony was still there, and, so that she would not bump
into either of them on the way back, Candra stayed out
much longer than usual.

It was almost dark when she did return; the MG had
gone and the house was in darkness. Were they out

together? The thought hurt far more than she expected, and she asked herself why when she had deliberately shut men out of her life, especially domineering men like him! The best thing she could do was forget Simeon. She would cancel Friday night, she would call off the race next Sunday, and she would avoid him like the plague in future.

But the second she stepped on to *Four Seasons*, the second Skye and Lady raced excitedly inside and she heard his voice, Candra knew it was not going to be that easy.

She rushed after the dogs, ready for instant battle, but he forestalled her. 'That was a very rude thing to do, Candra.' The harsh lines were back on his face.

'And it's very rude of you to invite yourself on to my boat,' she countered. 'Obviously I shall have to lock up every time I leave it for more than a few seconds.'

His eyes glittered angrily. 'How do you think Briony felt?'

'Relieved, I would think,' said Candra sharply. 'And I notice it didn't take you long to change your affections.'

His mouth firmed. 'I could not totally ignore her.'

'Of course not,' she answered icily. 'But, if nothing else, it's taught me how free and easy you are with your kisses. I'll know to slap your face if you try it again.'

With one swift movement his fingers bit into her shoulders. 'Candra, I kissed you because I wanted to, for no other reason. And I still want to.'

His eyes met and held hers, and for one mesmeric moment Candra could not look away. Her heart began to bang painfully against her rib-cage, but fury superseded desire and, bringing her hands up between his arms, she knocked them away. Then, before he had got over her surprise attack, she lifted her hand and aimed it with all her strength at his face.

He caught her wrist easily, twisting her arm behind her and bringing her body up against his. With his other hand he gripped her chin, and there was blazing intensity in his eyes as he claimed her mouth.

The savage fury of his kiss sent sheer, unadulterated pleasure shivering through Candra's limbs. She did her best to remain passive, but it was impossible when desire clawed at her stomach, and within seconds she was melting against him, her lips parting beneath his onslaught, her free arm winding itself around him.

Immediately his kiss gentled, and his fingers left her chin to trace the outline of her lips and feel the soft contours of her face. He let go of her wrist, his hand sliding up her back to her nape, burying itself in the thickness of her corn-coloured hair.

Candra wished she had the strength to stop him, but the tantalising torture of his kisses was driving her crazy with desire. This was something that had never happened to her before, and why this man? This man who had gone against her wishes to build on her grandfather's land, this man who had brought her here against her will. He was turning her world upside-down and there was not a thing she could do about it.

When his hand slid beneath her shirt and cupped her breast, Candra gave an involuntary whimper of pleasure. All thoughts of Briony had fled; her mind was filled with Simeon to the oblivion of all else. Finally he lifted his mouth to whisper fiercely, 'I hope that's proof enough?'

'Proof of what?' She tried to make her tone hard, and

must have succeeded because he frowned and let her go altogether.

'That I wasn't kissing you because I'd got nothing better to do. You're a fascinating, attractive woman, and I want to get to know you better.'

'I bet you do,' said Candra coldly. 'The same as you enjoy getting to know Briony. I don't know what your game is, but I'm not interested.'

An eyebrow lifted. 'That isn't what your body told me.'

'Bodies can be traitorous things,' she snapped. 'It's not easy to suppress sexual attraction, but that's all it is. You'd be a fool if you read anything else into it.'

'Of course.' The mockery was there again. 'I keep forgetting that you've locked your heart away and put your career first.

Candra's eyes flashed angrily. 'It's not only that.'

'Oh, I know,' he said with some amusement, 'you think all men treat women as slaves.'

'Well, don't you?'

'There's only one way you'll find out,' he grinned. 'I suggest we begin the voyage of discovery on Friday night.'

Candra was trapped by her renegade body. Her mind protested, but her body was pitifully weak. 'I'll go out with you,' she said slowly, 'but only because I lost the bet. I have no intention of making a habit of it.'

'We'll see.' His smile was confident as he left, and Candra felt like swinging a punch at him, but she knew who would be the loser if she dared.

Thankfully she saw nothing more of Simeon during the next two days, and on Wednesday she invited Andrew back for a meal. Ever since she'd moved he had been angling for an invitation, and she thought that perhaps now was the time. He followed her in his own car, parking behind her on the driveway to the house.

This was the only part of the arrangement that Candra did not like, because it meant that Simeon could see her coming and going. She wished there were somewhere else she could leave her car, but the lane outside was too narrow, and in all fairness the drive was big enough to accommodate a dozen cars.

He was not yet home, but he would be later, and certainly before Andrew went, and Candra imagined that he would be watching to see who her visitor was.

The dogs were waiting as they got out of their cars, tails wagging furiously, tongues lolling. Andrew duly fussed them.

'This is some place,' he said admiringly, looking around him as they walked along the pathway to *Four Seasons*. 'Have you been in the house? Is it as magnificent inside as it looks from here?'

'I've not seen all of it,' admitted Candra. 'But yes, I would say it's impressive.'

'And the people who live here, are they nice?'

She nodded, and was glad they had reached the boat so that further questioning was cut short. It was hot inside, and she opened doors and windows, and Andrew peeled potatoes while she put the chops under the grill and laid the table.

'How long do you plan living here?' he asked.

Candra shrugged. 'Till I get fed up, I suppose.'

'Don't you ever get lonely?'

She shook her head. 'Never. I've got the dogs.'

'They're company, yes,' he frowned, 'but you can hardly hold a conversation with them. Do you see much of the folks from the house?'

Here it was again, the question she had been dreading. 'Not a lot.'

'They leave you very much to yourself?'

Candra nodded.

'It's strange. I thought they'd be more sociable.'

'It's the way I like it,' said Candra sharply.

He frowned again as he looked at her. 'Don't you get on with them? Isn't it working out?'

'Yes, of course it is,' said Candra quickly. 'But I live my life and he—they live theirs.'

'He?' queried Andrew, quickly picking up her mistake.

'The man of the house. Actually, there's no woman there, and——'

'No woman?' cut in Andrew fiercely. 'What do you mean? You told me that——'

'I didn't tell you anything, you assumed it,' she interjected, her tone sharp. 'Let's forget it, Andrew; it's of no importance.'

'Not to you, maybe, but to me it is. You're very vulnerable here. I want to know who he is, what he's like, whether you're—safe. Is he old? Young?' He put down the knife and took her by the shoulders. 'Candra, you must tell me.'

She wrenched free and glared at him fiercely. 'Andrew, I told you, it doesn't matter. Just drop it, will you? He's a fine man, he won't hurt me. I'm perfectly safe. Have you finished those potatoes.'

She was protesting too much, she knew that, but Andrew had no right questioning her like this.

'You're hiding something.' His eyes behind his glasses fixed on her suspiciously. 'You don't want me to know about him, that's why you've been reluctant to let me come here. Candra, I always respected the fact that you didn't want to be rushed, but if there's someone who's managed to get through to you when I haven't, I think I deserve to know.'

'Andrew,' Candra led him to a seat and sat him down, 'this man means nothing at all to me. You must believe that.'

'But you do see him?'

'Occasionally. Not often.'

'I can find out, you know,' he said. 'I only have to ask Simeon Sterne.'

Candra nodded, and she knew that Andrew would not let go until he found out who lived in the house.

'I'll see him tomorrow.'

'No, Andrew,' she said quietly. 'There's no need. I'll tell you. It's Simeon himself.'

Andrew's brows drew together in a ferocious frown. 'Simeon Sterne? You're actually moored on his property?'

'Not his, exactly,' she informed him. 'It belongs to a friend of his. He's using it while his own house is being renovated.'

'*The swine!*'

Candra was shocked by the venom in Andrew's voice.

'You know what his game is, don't you?'

'No, I don't know what his game is,' she retorted. 'There is none, as far as I'm concerned. He made me a perfectly reasonable offer, and I would have been a fool to refuse. You admitted yourself that it's a perfect spot.'

'That was before I knew he lived here. I don't like it, Candra. Not one little bit. I'm going to find you somewhere else. I thought you hated the guy?'

Candra shrugged. 'He's all right. I'm not going to move, Andrew. I'm happy here.'

'I bet you are,' he sneered.

She frowned. 'What's that supposed to mean?'

'He's a fine-looking man, wealthy, available. He has much more going for him than me. You're on to a good thing.'

Candra eyed Andrew savagely. 'That's disgusting.'

'Something's changed in you, Candra. Even if you can't see it, I can. I think I'm wasting my time.'

Her tone softened. 'I never gave you any false hopes, Andrew.'

'But I did hope. Why do you think I stuck around?' His eyes were sad behind his glasses. 'I thought while there was no one else there would always be hope for me. But Simeon Sterne? I don't like it. He has a reputation for being hard and ruthless. Hasn't his wife died? From what I've heard, he's been even more difficult since.'

'He is,' agreed Candra.

'Yet you're still prepared to live here?'

'I don't live in his pocket. I live my own life, and he lives his. You're making an issue out of nothing, Andrew.'

And with that he had to be satisfied.

CHAPTER SIX

WHEN Simeon came to the boat for Candra on Friday evening, it was the first time she had seen him since the weekend. Even as she dressed—in a blue and green silk dress with a swirling skirt and shoestring straps—she hoped he would forget. She kept telling herself that she did not want to see him, and yet the instant he appeared she felt the now familiar quickening of her pulses.

He wore an off-white jacket and black trousers, with a black shirt and white tie, and he looked more devilishly handsome than ever. As she stepped off the boat, he steadied her, and the touch of his hand on her elbow set every nerve quivering. Nor did he let her go as they walked to his car. 'I'm glad you didn't change your mind about coming.'

'I was rather hoping you would,' she said abruptly

Simeon's hand tightened and he drew in a swift breath, but he said nothing until she was settled in the BMW. 'Why did you invite Andrew back to your boat? I thought no man was welcome.'

'Andrew doesn't pressurise me,' she told me quietly.

'He's solid, safe and dependable, is that the sum of it?' He swore beneath his breath and crashed a gear. 'Whereas I am bad-tempered, unpredictable and totally domineering.'

'There's a lot to be said for dependability,' she returned coolly.

Again another whistle through his teeth. 'And for men who don't boss you around. Go on, you might as well say it. Do you plan to marry this paragon of virtue?'

'I don't plan to marry anyone,' she retorted, 'not for a long time. But when I do it might well be Andrew, or someone like him.'

Simeon stamped on the brakes as a dog ran across the road, and his knuckles gleamed white as he gripped the steering-wheel. 'Dammit, Candra, you'd be bored out of your tiny mind within weeks. Are you seriously saying that you prefer someone like that?'

'To someone like you, yes. I've had enough of men trying to dominate me.'

He gave an impatient toss of his head, and an uncomfortable silence settled between them. Candra could see the evening stretching miserably ahead.

Hey House was a recently converted private home, part of it dating back to the fourteenth century. It was set in five acres of landscaped grounds, and backed on to the canal. It had a relaxing, intimate atmosphere, and Candra wished things were different between them. It could have been a most enjoyable evening.

He ordered drinks, and they sat sipping them in the lounge before being taken through to their table in the Victorian-style conservatory overlooking the water. It was an idyllic setting, quite out of this world, and yet Simeon had scowled at the menu and now he was scowling at her. Was he jealous of Andrew? Was that what was wrong? It didn't make sense, and yet what other reason could there be for his odd behaviour?

'I don't think this is a very good idea,' she said tightly. 'I'd like you to take me home.'

He looked at her, and suddenly his face softened and he smiled. And everything changed. Candra felt a quickening of her pulses. That was all it took; a smile.

The world was once again a happy place. Then she realised that he was not looking at her, but over her shoulder. Instinctively she turned—and saw Briony! A chill crawled down her spine.

'Excuse me,' he said, rising immediately and going over to the other girl. Anger boiled up inside Candra. How insufferably rude! She watched them as they spoke, and Simeon appeared to be inviting Briony to join them. What a nerve! She clenched her fists and turned quickly away. She would go. She would leave immediately. No way was she going to sit here and watch them billing and cooing.

But before she could move Simeon's hand touched her shoulder. 'I hope you don't mind, Candra, but I've asked Briony to join us?' There was more warmth in his voice than she had heard all evening.

Yes, I do mind. I mind very much, she said under her breath, but she merely shrugged and tried to smile. It was hard. 'Feel free.'

Within a matter of seconds a waiter appeared, another place was set and Candra was trapped. If the evening had been uncomfortable before, now it was going to be hell.

Briony wore a white strapless dress which starkly contrasted with her honeyed skin and black hair. 'I had a date, but he let me down at the last minute,' she explained, 'and I didn't see why I should stay in. I had no idea you two would be here.'

Candra did not believe her. Simeon had probably told Briony their plans, and she had deliberately set out to ruin them. What the girl did not know was that the evening was ruined already.

Simeon gave no indication that they were barely on

speaking terms, doing his best to involve both girls in the conversation. Briony, though, had other ideas. She constantly spoke about friends and situations of which Candra had no knowledge, and when Candra went to the Ladies' Briony followed. 'You're wasting your time where Simeon is concerned,' she said at once.

Candra dabbed powder on her nose and looked at her coolly through the mirror. 'Really?'

'You're not the sort who appeals to him.'

'And you are, I suppose?' Candra asked waspishly.

'But of course. Has he told you about his wife?'

Candra nodded, taking a comb out of her bag and dragging it unnecessarily through her hair.

'She was my best friend.'

That did surprise Candra. Her eyes widened and she paused a moment, looking at the other girl, who was busy applying another layer of bright red lipstick.

'When we met Simeon, we both fell in love with him.'

'And now Marie's dead you're hoping he'll turn to you?'

'Not hoping, I know,' said Briony sharply. 'It's all a matter of time, of course.'

Candra's brows rose. 'I thought he was over her. What's he waiting for if he loves you?'

Briony's eyes narrowed spitefully. 'If you hadn't turned up he'd have popped the question by now, I'm sure of it.'

'I apologise if I'm in the way,' Candra retorted drily. 'But it was his suggestion that I move my boat to the bottom of his garden.

'I don't mind that,' snapped Briony, 'so long as you keep yourself to yourself.'

'As a matter of fact, that would suit me fine.' Candra's tone was icy cold. 'It's Simeon who has other ideas. Perhaps he's not so fond of you as you think.'

Briony's eyes flashed her hatred. 'That's a lie. Simeon loves me.'

'And yet he asked me out tonight?' Candra could not help taunting the other girl.

'Only because of that silly, stupid bet. He told me all about it.'

'Then you must know that, whoever won, we would have ended up coming out together. Doesn't that suggest something to you, Briony?'

The other girl lifted her chin haughtily. 'It suggests that Simeon's a gentleman. He probably felt sorry for you. But you'd be ill-advised to read anything into it.'

'Of course he's a gentleman,' returned Candra. 'Otherwise he wouldn't have asked you to join us. Perhaps it's you he feels sorry for?' And with that she turned and swept out of the room. Not for anything was she going to give Briony the satisfaction of knowing how she felt about Simeon, or any other domineering man like him.

Briony followed and they sat down together. Simeon looked at Candra's flushed face curiously, but said nothing, and a few minutes later he suggested they leave, surprising her by insisting on settling the bill himself.

'But I lost the bet,' she protested. 'I really don't mind.'

'I mind,' he informed her. 'You never really thought I'd let you pay? I've never let a girl pay for me in my life.'

Briony listened to them with something approaching

boredom, and when they went out to the car she asked
Simeon whether he would give her a lift home. Before
he had even answered she slid into the front seat. 'I came
in a taxi,' she explained, confirming Candra's
suspicions that she had known they would be here.

When Briony realised he was heading in the direction
of her house, she put her hand on his leg and said at
once, 'There's no rush, Simeon. Take Candra home
first, and then come back for coffee. My parents are
away, we'll have the house to ourselves.'

'Some other time, perhaps,' he said, with a softening
smile.

Candra sensed the girl's anger, but Briony had the
good sense not to create a scene. When they arrived,
however, Briony sat and waited for him to open her
door, and then made sure he saw her into the house. In
the front porch she openly kissed him, and Candra
turned her head away, suddenly hurt at the sight of
another girl in his arms, though she could not explain
why. She didn't want him herself, did she? So why did
it matter?

And when he insisted she take Briony's place in the
front seat, she sat with her hands clasped primly in her
lap, her eyes looking straight ahead.

'I'm sorry if Briony's presence disturbed you,' he
said. 'But I couldn't let her eat by herself.'

'Of course not,' returned Candra mildly.

Her tone did not deceive him. 'What were you talking
about in the cloakroom? You came back looking ready
to do battle. I hoped you two would be good friends.'

'She's your friend, not mine,' she told him. 'And, if
you must know, I was being warned off.'

He smiled. 'That sounds typical Briony. She's a very

possessive person. What did you say to her?'

Candra shrugged. 'Actually I let her think there was something going on between us. I don't take kindly to threats.'

To her surprise, he grinned. 'I'd have been disappointed if you'd reacted otherwise. It's what I've come to expect from you, Candra.'

She noticed he did not deny that there was something going on between him and Briony, but as far as she was concerned he was welcome to her. Perhaps Briony liked to be dominated?

They reached the house, and he stopped the car and half turned in his seat towards her. The security light had come on and it was almost like daylight. 'You know something, Candra, you're quite a girl.'

'I am what I am,' she told him flatly.

'You're unlike anyone else I've ever met.'

'A curiosity'

'A very desirable woman.'

He inched slowly towards her, and Candra pushed herself back against the door, her fingers on the handle ready for a quick escape. It was obvious kisses meant nothing to him—he handed them out as freely as one would a bag of toffees. 'Keep away from me, Simeon.' There was a hint of panic in her voice, even though every nerve vibrated with excitement at the thought of him touching her.

A frown fixed itself between his eyebrows. 'Candra, I'm not going to hurt you, for Pete's sake.'

'You should have dropped me off first and gone home with Briony. Or is it because she's easy and you enjoy a battle? It that it? Is that what's attracting you to me? Whatever, Simeon, I'm not into affairs. You know that.

Just keep your hands off me.'

'I want more from you than an affair, Candra,' he said, taking her shoulders and looking deeply into her eyes. 'Haven't you understood that yet?'

Her whole body became a mass of sensation, her eyes widened into liquid green pools.It was an effort to hold herself rigid; it was an effort even to breathe. 'I don't particularly care what you want.' She intended to speak sharply, instead her voice sounded slightly breathless. 'Any sort of a relationship has to be two-sided, and this isn't, and never will be. Will you please let me go?'

'You're making a big mistake, Candra.'

'And yours is even bigger if you think I'll ever respond to you. Give Briony your kisses, just leave me alone. I don't want you in my life, not now, not ever. Don't you understand that?'

His hands suddenly fell from her shoulders. 'It's Andrew, isn't it? Dear, solid, dependable Andrew, who never asks anything from you that you're not prepared to give. Hell, what a waste.'

Candra did not bother to answer. Finding herself free, she scrambled out of the car and sped across the lawn. A second security light came on, illuminating her way. Even so, she stumbled a couple of times in her haste before reaching the boat.

The dogs barked as she fumbled with her key, almost knocking her over as they tried to get out. Knowing she would have difficulty in sleeping, Candra poured herself a generous measure of brandy and carried it through to her bedroom, taking a mouthful before she undressed and cleaned off her make-up, and the rest once the dogs were safely in and she had slid into bed. She lay down and pulled the covers over her, and in seconds was asleep.

The next morning Candra hoped and prayed she would not see Simeon. Why was he making things so difficult? Why wouldn't he take no for an answer? She felt she was being trapped into a situation for which she was not ready. Men like Simeon held no appeal for her. Couldn't he understand that?

Maybe she ought to go out for the day? She had her weekly shopping to do, and she could visit her parents. She would take the dogs with her—they would enjoy that.

She pulled on a leisure-suit and accompanied Skye and Lady on their usual morning romp in the woods. Afterwards she showered and put on a summer dress, ate a slice of toast and drank a cup of coffee, then locked up carefully. So far, so good.

As she crossed the lawn, Candra carefully avoided looking at the house. She quickly manoeuvred herself and the dogs inside the car, but when she turned her key in the ignition nothing happened. She tried again. Still nothing. And again.

In desperation, she got out and lifted the bonnet. But she really had no idea what she was looking for. There were no obvious loose wires, everything seemed intact.

'Something wrong?'

The deep voice behind made her jump. Candra turned and met Simeon's eyes, and to her annoyance her heart leapt. She took refuge in anger, tightening her lips and glaring at him coldly. 'Nothing that I can't sort out, thank you very much.'

He wore a pair of faded jeans this morning, and a yellow T-shirt that moulded itself to his muscular body. His eyes were bright and clear, and he looked as though he had been up for hours. He pursed his lips. 'A car mechanic as well, eh? The complete feminist. Is there nothing you can't do?'

The sarcasm in his voice fanned Candra's anger. 'Not a lot.'

'I'm glad to hear it.' And with that he turned and walked back into the house.

Candra wished she had not been so uptight. She hadn't the slightest idea what was wrong, and now she had lost any chance of help. Then she remembered when her father's car had developed the same problem. The starter motor had stuck. He had rocked the car and it had done the trick.

Using all her strength, she leaned on the bonnet and bounced the car up and down. She felt very foolish because she guessed Simeon would be watching from the house. Then she jumped inside and turned the key. When again it wouldn't start, she clenched her fists and banged them on the steering-wheel.

Again Simeon appeared. 'Still having trouble?'

'What does it look like?' she riposted.

'Turn the key, let me listen.'

Much against her will, Candra obeyed.

'It's your starter motor.'

'Thank you, but I know that,' she informed him drily.

'It could be jammed.'

'I've already rocked the car.'

His lips quirked. 'Yes, I saw you.'

Candra glared. 'Then you have a go.'

He did so with seemingly effortless ease, but still without result. 'Where are you going?' he asked.

'Shopping.'

'I'll give you a lift.'

She ignored him. 'And then I was going to pay my parents a visit. I planned to stay the day.'

'There's still no reason why you shouldn't. I'm at your disposal.'

Candra frowned. 'You don't have to give up your time for me.'

'No, I don't have to,' he answered levelly, 'but I want to. Give me a minute to get changed and we'll go.'

'How about the dogs?' Candra could not imagine he would like them in his BMW.

'I'm sure they'll behave. I'll put a blanket on the back seat.'

He was gone before she could protest further, and Candra had no recourse but to get out of her car and lock it up. The dogs sat at her heels, as if wondering what was going to happen next. They had been excited at the prospect of a car journey. They loved them. And now that they had been forced to get out again they were confused.

But within a couple of minutes Simeon was back. Smart grey trousers this time, and a pink shirt. 'Give me your keys,' he said, holding out his hand.

Frowningly, Candra handed them to him. He took them into the house and dropped them on to the hall table. 'Why have you done that?' she asked.

'I phoned the garage. They'll be here shortly. Pauline will give them the keys. When you come back tonight your car will be fixed.'

On a Saturday? When most people finished at lunchtime? His name obviously carried a lot of weight. What could she say, but thank you? 'It's very kind of you, Simeon. I'm grateful.'

'It's the least I can do,' he said offhandedly as he

opened his passenger door.

It was impossible when she was inside not to feel vaguely uneasy. He was intruding into her life whether she wanted him to or not. No matter how often or how firmly she told herself that she did not want to get involved, that he was the type of man she abhorred most, she felt herself responding. His magnetism was total.

Candra did not realise how tightly she was holding her bag until Simeon said, 'What are you thinking?'

Honesty had always been Candra's policy, so she said abruptly, 'About last night.'

'Briony?'

'Partly, I suppose.'

'What else?'

'The fact that you want more from me than I'm prepared to give.'

'And that bothers you, does it?' He glanced across at her as he slowed for a set of lights.

'Naturally. And I fail to understand why you persist when you've got Briony ready to jump into your bed.'

He was silent a moment, then he said, 'It doesn't always pay to let your head rule your heart.'

Candra gave a soft laugh. 'There's no fear of that. You're the type of man I loathe most.'

He gave a sudden snort of anger. 'You're persecuting yourself.'

'I don't think so,' she said quietly but firmly. 'And I see no point at all in this conversation. I have no real interest in you, and you, if you're perfectly honest, will admit that you have none in me. By your own admittance I intrigue you, but that is all. So will you please leave me alone?'

Thankfully they reached Stonely and he drove on to

the supermarket car park. When he cut the engine and also prepared to get out, Candra protested. 'Thank you, Simeon, for the lift, but I'll catch a bus to my parents'. You needn't wait.'

'As it happens,' he said, 'I need to do some shopping too.'

Candra was not sure that she believed him, but what could she say? They left the car windows open for the dogs, and he accompanied her into the supermarket. Skye and Lady were used to going shopping and would not get out of the car, nor would anyone dare touch it while they were inside.

They used the same trolley, and his shopping consisted of a tube of toothpaste and a bag of toffees. 'I have a weakness for them,' he confessed.

Candra found it strange being accompanied up and down the shopping aisles by a man. It had never happened to her before. He raised an eyebrow when she put several tubes of mints into the trolley. 'Is that your weakness?'

He was her weakness, she thought. And the more she saw of him, the harder it would be to deny that he meant anything to her. Even amid all these people, she could still feel the tug of his magnetism. 'They're for Skye and Lady,' she answered. 'And the horse in the field opposite your friend's house. He comes to me every morning when I walk the dogs.'

'Does he now?' asked Simeon with a quirk of his thick brows. 'Maybe I ought to join you. I like horses. Do you ride? No, forget I asked that question. Of course you ride. You're a woman of many talents.'

Candra was not sure whether or not he was mocking her, so she frowned, but kept her mouth shut.

'I have a friend who owns a farm and has a couple of horses who could use some exercise. We'll go together one day.'

Candra doubted it. Her feelings where Simeon was concerned were growing far too quickly, and the earlier she stamped on them, the better.

But there was no getting away from him. He insisted on driving her to her parents' converted farm cottage on the outskirts of Hey. It had originally been a one-up, one-down cottage, but now there were three bedrooms, a large living-room, a dining-room and a kitchen. The gardens weren't big, but they were well-tended with a pleasant square of lawn and a rose-bed, as well as Mr Drake's vegetable garden.

Simeon pulled up outside and Candra turned to him. 'Thank you so much, Simeon. You've been very kind.'

'Am I dismissed?' he asked. 'Do I not get an introduction to your parents? Surely they'd be interested in meeting the man who lives so—what shall I say—so dangerously close to their daughter?'

Before Candra could answer her mother came hurrying down the path. She was of the same height as Candra, with the same open features, and her hair was still remarkably dark for her age. She was slim and elegant, and she leaned through Candra's open window and kissed her daughter's cheek.

The dogs pushed their noses towards her as well, and she duly fussed them, but her attention was riveted on the man at Candra's side. 'Candra, love, what a nice surprise. And who is this? Don't tell me you've got yourself a boyfriend at last?'

'Mother!' muttered Candra warningly. 'This is Mr Sterne. He's kindly given me a lift because my car won't start.'

Mrs Drake frowned. 'Oh, dear. I hope it's nothing serious. Mr Sterne? Is he the man who bought your grandfather's land?'

Candra found it distinctly embarrassing that her mother was speaking about Simeon as though he weren't there, but Simeon seemed to find the whole thing amusing. He leaned across Candra and held out his hand. 'The very same. Simeon Sterne. I'm pleased to meet you, Mrs Drake. It's easy to see where Candra got her good looks from.'

The woman was hooked. 'You must come in, Mr Sterne, and meet my husband. I admit I was worried when Candra told us about you, but now I can see that it was entirely unfounded.'

Candra wished the floor would open and swallow her up. She dared a glance at Simeon, and he was smiling his satisfaction. 'Perhaps you ought to tell your daughter that? Sometimes I think she doesn't trust me.'

'She's choosy, that's all,' said Mrs Drake drily, opening the door so that Candra could get out.

Candra knew her mother was disappointed that she had not yet married, but she wished she would not make it so obvious. They both followed her up the path to the cottage, and Candra sensed Simeon's amusement. It was there in his relaxed stride, the way he was gently humming to himself. She was furious.

'David!' Indoors Mrs Drake summoned her husband.

He appeared with a frown on his face, which turned to a smile when he saw his daughter. 'It's good to see you, girl, you don't come often enough. Who's this you've brought with you?'

'Simeon Sterne,' introduced Candra.

'The man who found her somewhere to keep her boat,' added her mother.

Simeon held out his hand, and her father shook it firmly. 'Also the man who forced her to move, I believe?'

'All in the line of business,' said Simeon.

'I believe she gave you a hard time?'

'She's certainly a spirited lady,' he admitted.

'Always has been,' agreed the older man. 'Never takes kindly to orders. But she's a good girl, nevertheless——'

'Candra's having trouble with her car,' cut in Mrs Drake.

David frowned. 'What's wrong with it?'

'The starter motor,' answered Simeon.

'I might have a spare one in the garage,' said David. 'I'll have a look in a minute.'

'It's not necessary,' replied Simeon. 'I've already called out Mollet's.'

'On a Saturday?' David's brows rose.

Simeon shrugged. 'They do a lot of work for me, they don't mind.'

Mr Drake looked impressed, and Candra realised that he, surprisingly, approved of Simeon. Which was something of a record. No other man she had taken home had been good enough for his daughter. In fact, they had all been so intimidated by him that Candra had never seen them again. Only Craig had not seemed worried by him.

'Mum, do you think I could put some of my shopping in your freezer?' she asked.

'Of course, love,' said the woman at once.

'I'll fetch it for you,' offered Simeon.

'No, thanks,' replied Candra politely. 'You stay and talk to my father.' As she walked out of the room, she heard her father ask him whether he would like a pint, and she smiled to herself. Simeon was a whisky man.

To her surprise, however, when she returned to the house the two men had glasses of beer in their hands, and Simeon was telling her father about his new development. David was listening avidly, particularly interested in the marina, throwing in the odd comment, nodding his agreement. Simeon was outlining his plans in far more detail than he ever had to her, thought Candra bitterly.

'How can you agree with him,' she asked her father, 'when, not only is he going against everything Gramps fought for, but he also caused me and all the other boat owners to move? We liked it there. We didn't want to go.'

'I didn't like you being there,' said her father abruptly. 'Anyone could have been lurking inside those empty warehouses. But it didn't matter what I thought, did it? Got too big for your boots all of a sudden. Simeon's doing a good job in making something out of what is nothing more than an eyesore.'

Candra flashed her eyes hostilely. 'A nature reserve would have been prettier.'

'Progress is inevitable, and your mother and I feel much happier now you've moved.'

'I was safe enough with the dogs,' she retorted. 'Nothing ever happened to me.'

'You were lucky,' clipped her father.

Simeon nodded. 'I agree. And please, both of you, feel free to visit her whenever you wish. Any friend or member of Candra's family is welcome.'

Except Andrew, thought Candra. She glanced at Simeon and met his eyes—and he knew what she was thinking. His mouth lifted at the corners, so slightly that only she noticed.

'You will be staying to lunch, Simeon?' enquired Mrs Drake.

Candra shook her head. 'No, he's——'

Simeon cut her short. 'Yes, I'd love to, Mrs Drake.'

Candra glared. Mrs Drake smiled. 'Good. And call me Pamela, please. If you'll excuse me, I'll get started. Candra, will you give me a hand?'

In the kitchen Mrs Drake said, 'What a nice man. I'm glad you're getting on with him at last, and I feel much happier now that I've met him too.'

'Don't read anything into it,' said Candra quickly. 'I'm not ready to settle down with any man, particularly Simeon. He's not my type at all. I hate what he's doing to Gramps' land. Besides, he already has a girlfriend.'

'That's a pity,' said her mother. 'You and he would make an ideal couple. I'm surprised he's not already married.'

'He was,' admitted Candra. 'His wife died a few years ago.'

'Oh, Candra, love, how sad. The poor man. This girl he's seeing, is it serious?'

Candra could not help smiling. 'You never give up, do you, Mum?'

'Correct me if I'm wrong, Candra, but I sense that you feel more for him than you're admitting?'

Her mother knew her too well. 'Maybe I do,' she shrugged, 'but it won't ever lead to anything. I won't let it.'

'Because of this other girl?'

'Because he's too damn bossy, that's why. Don't you think I had enough of Daddy trying to rule my life without letting someone else do it as well? Mum, you don't know what he's like. He's already made me do things I didn't want to do. Whatever I feel for him has to stay buried.'

'Love doesn't die easily,' informed her mother.

'Who's talking about love?' demanded Candra. 'You really are jumping the gun, aren't you? I don't love Simeon.'

Footsteps behind made her whirl. Both her father and Simeon stood there, empty beer glasses in their hands, but it was Simeon's eyes that met hers.

CHAPTER SEVEN

IF SIMEON had heard Candra's statement that she did not love him, he gave no indication. His eyes locked into hers for a long, timeless moment, and her pulses raced, but when her father spoke he looked away.

'We've come for a refill,' said David, 'then I'm going to show Simeon the garden.'

Pamela nodded. 'Would you mind getting me a cabbage while you're out there?'

They filled their glasses from Mr Drake's barrel of home-made beer and made their way outside. Candra watched as her father pointed out his favourite roses, Simeon showing exactly the right amount of interest. It amazed her how well these two men were getting on together, though perhaps it shouldn't have done, considering they were of the same breed.

Her mother unconsciously reiterated her thoughts. 'It's nice they're getting on so well.'

'What's nice about it?' asked Candra sharply. 'There's no chance they'll meet again.'

Pamela gave a secretive smile. 'A little bird told me that you went out to dinner with Simeon Sterne last night.'

Candra gasped, wondering how news could travel so fast. 'Who was that?'

'Mary Lyle.'

'I might have known. Is there anything that woman doesn't know? Who told her?'

'Nora Brown, I think,' admitted her mother. 'She was

117

at Hey House last night. Naturally, I didn't recognise who it was when she described him, but now I can see that it was Simeon. Tall, black-haired, incredibly good-looking, driving a BMW. I was asked if you were going to get married—*at long last*.' Pamela emphasised the three words with distaste.

'I hope you told her to mind her own business?' snapped Candra.

'People will talk, and I must admit that I'm worried. When I was your age I was married with two children.'

'There's plenty of time,' retorted Candra. 'I shall get married when I'm good and ready, and not before. I happen to like my independence.'

Mrs Drake wisely said no more.

Lunch was a lively affair, with David Drake regaling Simeon with tales about when he was a boy accompanying his father on his narrow-boat. 'Times were different then, my lad. There were no pleasure boats. It was all work. Damned hard work.'

'I appreciate that,' said Simeon.

'Nevertheless, the old boatmen loved every minute. It was their way of life. Most of them had never known anything else, wouldn't have wanted anything else.'

They continued to talk about canals and boating well into the afternoon, and it was almost four when Candra suggested they leave.

'I'll be seeing you, David,' Simeon said, shaking her father's hand.

Candra hoped it was a figure of speech.

Then Simeon kissed Pamela's cheek. 'Thank you very much for your hospitality. The lunch was delicious.'

'You must come again,' she said, her eyes shining.

'And I expect you, Candra, to visit us more often,' admonished her father as he gave her a brief hug.

'I'll try,' said Candra, but she could take only so much of her father. Today hadn't been too bad, he'd had Simeon to divert him, but normally she bore the brunt of his displeasure.

'I'm sorry my father monopolised you,' she said, once they were on their way. 'I'm afraid he doesn't know when to stop once he gets going.'

'Don't apologise,' Simeon replied at once. 'He's a most interesting man. I could have listened to him all day. It's a pity you don't get on. I think perhaps you don't fully understand him.'

'Oh, I understand him all right,' she returned brittly. 'The same as I understand you. Neither of you is happy unless you're in charge. He has my mother running around him like a little slave. That's not for me, I'm afraid.'

His mouth firmed, but he said no more, and the journey home took only ten minutes. The dogs jumped out the second the doors were opened, racing down to the boat and back, tails wagging furiously. Candra's car had been moved; it was tucked neatly into a corner of the drive. 'It looks as if Mollet's got it going,' remarked Simeon.

Candra nodded. 'You must let me have the bill.'

'I told them to charge it to my account.'

Her eyes widened. 'Oh, no, I——'

'If you insist, you can pay me back,' he said, 'but it doesn't matter. Let's say it was a favour to a—platonic friend.'

The slight hesitation told Candra quite clearly that he had heard her declaration. Her cheeks coloured, and she hid her face in the boot as she reached for her bags.

'I'll carry your shopping,' said Simeon, his voice close to her ear.

She could not ignore the warmth that ran through her. All day she had made a careful effort to show indifference, but now the hours spent together were beginning to tell on her. Her body, if not her mind, was responding to his, her pulses racing, her heartbeats quickening. 'Thank you.' Even her voice sounded different.

'It seems to me,' he said as they walked along the path, 'that you've enough here to feed an army. Are you expecting company?'

Candra shook her head. 'I like to keep well stocked, just in case.'

'In case of what?'

'Anything,' she said. 'It's not as if there's a corner shop I can run to.'

His eyes narrowed. 'You mean if someone like Andrew calls?'

The difference in his tone was distinctly noticeable—it was almost accusing—but Candra chose to ignore it. 'That's right,' she said brightly.

They reached the boat and she opened the doors, then turned to take her bags off him. 'Thank you, Simeon, for all you've done today.'

She was descending carefully, backwards, down the steps, when he called out to her. 'Don't forget tomorrow, Candra.'

Tomorrow? A frown scoured her brow. She put the bags down on the floor and went back up. 'What about tomorrow?'

'The swimming race. Have you forgotten that you

threw out another challenge?'

Candra had forgotten, and she wished that he had as well. But she nodded all the same. 'It still stands, unless you've invited Briony again. I have no particular wish to perform in front of her.'

'No, I haven't invited Briony,' he told her impatiently. 'Let's say about twelve. The loser provides lunch.'

He was mighty fond of instigating penalties, thought Candra. But, nevertheless, it would be interesting to eat something that he had prepared. 'In which case I hope you're a good cook,' she said drily.

When he had gone Candra busied herself putting away her purchases. She had planned today so that she would not see Simeon, and instead had spent it with him. She felt, although she hated to admit it, warm and bubbly and vitally alive. She felt different. And when she looked in the mirror her eyes were sparkling and there was an unusual glow to her face. She could not remember any other man affecting her in this way—and it had happened without her realising it—*and against her will*.

On an impulse, she untied the boat and set out along the canal. She enjoyed these lone trips. It was another world completely. The water was glassy-smooth today, reflecting the graceful willows and grasses that grew along the canal-sides. The mirror-image was rippled by her slow-moving boat, leaving behind a gentle wake of moving water and bubbles.

Ahead, on the towpath, stood a heron, perfectly still, white neck outstretched, watching, waiting. But before she reached him he soared into the sky, his movements slow and majestic, circling, coming back to rest behind her.

A little further on in the reeds was a family of moorhens, black with red foreheads, diminutive in relation to the heron.

She did not go far, winding at the first convenient spot and then heading back. Winding was a funny word, she contemplated. It was pronounced as in the wind that blew and had always amused her. Why couldn't they just say turning?

The short trip was sufficient to relax her, to give her peace of mind, to forget all her unwanted thoughts and desires where Simeon was concerned. But her contentment did not last long. The second she nosed her boat under the bridge she saw Simeon standing at the canal edge. Was he waiting for her? Or was he simply enjoying the early evening air? Whatever, it was sufficient to bring the butterflies back into her stomach.

Candra brought her boat neatly to the side, and Simeon tied up one end while she did the other. Not a word was spoken until it was secure. Then he said sharply, 'What made you take off like that?'

'I wanted to be alone,' she replied.

He frowned. 'But you're alone here.'

'It's different when you're actually moving. There's a serenity about it that I can't explain.'

'And you needed to be soothed, is that what you're saying?' he rasped. 'Why? I thought today went rather well. I thoroughly enjoyed meeting your parents. '

'And they enjoyed meeting you, I'm sure,' she returned crisply, stepping back on to her boat.

Simeon followed. 'It wouldn't by any chance have anything to do with the conversation you had with your mother?'

Candra drew in a swift breath, pausing in the act of stepping down inside. It took her a few seconds to compose her face. 'Nothing at all, Simeon. I'd forgotten all about it, as a matter of fact.'

His blue eyes met hers. 'Somehow I don't believe you. You made too profound a statement to forget it that easily.'

'It was of no importance,' said Candra, lifting her shoulders airily, glad he could not see the chaos he had created inside her.

'Saying that you don't love me was of no importance?' he enquired, one eyebrow raised disapprovingly. 'It's tantamount to saying that *I'm* of no importance. I'd like to know how the conversation started.'

'It's perfectly natural that my mother should ask questions. It's such a rare occurrence for me to turn up with a man.'

'Except Andrew, of course?'

Her chin lifted. 'Andrew has never been home with me.'

He pulled a surprised face. 'Maybe I should be thankful for small mercies.'

'You can be thankful for what the hell you like,' she snapped. 'If I'd had my way you wouldn't have gone with me today.'

His thick brows rose. 'It's a pity you're not as friendly as your parents.'

'They don't know you as I do.'

'They seem to approve of what I'm doing.'

Candra shrugged. 'That doesn't mean to say I have to.'

'And they also approve of the fact that you're living

so close to me. They like to think that I'm protecting you.'

'Some protection,' she scorned.

His eyes darkened. 'And what is that supposed to mean?'

'It means,' she flashed, anger getting the better of discretion, 'that you never lose an opportunity to kiss me, that all you seem to be after is——' When his fingers bit into her shoulders, she stopped. 'Simeon, you're hurting me.'

'Are you denying,' he asked coldly, 'that you feel a response? That you enjoy it? Are you?' He shook her as though she were a rag doll. 'Say yes, Candra, and I won't believe you.'

'Of course I feel something,' she gasped, 'but it's purely physical. It doesn't mean a thing.'

'It could if you'd let it. I can't make up my mind whether it's Andrew or your damned career that's standing between us.'

'Try Briony,' she crisped, and then wished she hadn't, because it wasn't only Briony who was stopping her.

A smile appeared. 'You're jealous?'

'I am not jealous,' she said tightly.

'Then it won't bother you that I'm seeing her tonight?'

'Not at all.'

'You're not a very good liar, Candra.' His hands were still on her shoulders and he pulled her closer to him. She tried to free herself, but in vain, and when his mouth closed on hers it would have been the easiest thing in the world to relax and respond and enjoy every second.

But for her own peace of mind she had to resist. And somehow she managed it. She fought him every inch of the way. Her body stiff, her mouth unyielding beneath his. Her insides on fire! Until in the end he thrust her savagely from him. 'Today you win,' he snarled. 'But there is always tomorrow. Today you were forewarned. Next time I'll choose my moment with more care.' He looked at her long and hard, then the next second she was free and he was walking back to the house.

Candra could still feel his hands on her shoulders and his lips on hers and an ache inside her. Why, she asked herself, was she fighting the attraction that she felt?

'Ready, set, *go*!'

As they dived cleanly into the water, Candra's only thought was that she had to beat this man. Thoughts of him had kept her awake most of the night, and if there had been any way she could have got out of this race she would have taken it, but cowardice was not one of her failings. She had walked across to the pool at half-past eleven and swum a few practice lengths.

Simeon himself had not come out of the house until a minute or so before twelve. Obviously he felt no need for a warm-up. 'Good morning, Candra,' he had called from the side of the pool. 'I've been watching you from the house. I trust you haven't worn yourself out? I should hate the race to be unfair.'

'You don't have to worry about me,' she replied, swimming towards him and accepting his helping hand as she climbed out.

He wore black swimming-trunks today, and Candra found her eyes drawn to his magnificent body, to muscular arms and legs and a deep powerful chest, to his hard, flat stomach with the arrowing of dark hairs that disappeared inside his trunks. All that power! What hope had she of beating him? It would take some doing, but even if it took every ounce of her strength she was determined to do it.

By the end of lap three they were still neck and neck. Each time they turned Simeon gave her a grin, his teeth gleaming white. Candra wondered whether he was reserving any of his energy, as she had done last week. She hoped not, because she was certainly putting her all into it.

Laps four, five, six and seven, and they were still level. Candra began to grow suspicious. One or other of them should have been ahead, even if only by a couple of seconds. He was doing it deliberately, she felt sure, and when on the eighth length she surged ahead of him, and at the end of it they were still level, she knew she was right. His grin was even wider.

Right, thought Candra, there was only one way out of this—go for it now. It was no good leaving it until the last moment. Although she was a very powerful swimmer, she was still a woman, and Simeon was much better than she had at first thought. She willed extra power into her arms and legs, finding resources that she had not known she possessed. This competition was very important to her.

She had no idea where Simeon was, even when she turned. She concentrated solely on swimming faster than she had ever done before. She pushed herself to her very limits, feeling the blood pounding in her head, concentrating, concentrating.

But it was not enough. At the end Simeon was a couple of seconds in front of her. Blue eyes met grey and his triumph was unmistakable. Bitter disappointment welled inside Candra as they each took a few moments to regain their breath. She had been so sure she could beat him, so very sure. Damn the man! Why did he have to be so good?

'My congratulations,' he said at length, and still there was that smile of triumph in his eyes.

Candra frowned aggressively, her breasts heaving from the exertion. 'What for?'

'Putting up such a good fight. You almost won.' He said it as though it were the most incredible thing in the world.

'But I didn't, did I?' she snapped, furiously angry with herself now for losing, especially by two seconds. She should have been able to do it, she should have pushed herself harder. And now, dammit, she had to cook him lunch.

And yet, even here in the water, completely exhausted, she was still aware of his overpowering sexuality. It cloaked him like a mantle at all times. She was trapped by it like a fawn in a beam of light. There was no escape.

With his black hair plastered to his well-shaped head, and the droplets of water shimmering like diamonds on his eyelashes and face and shoulders, he was totally, totally magnetic male and there was no ignoring him. She knew it would always be like this. She could go on telling herself that she hated him, that she wanted nothing to do with him, that he was the type of man she despised most, but it would do no good. The only way out of this situation would be to move her boat right away from here.

'Does it bother you that I won?' The thought seemed to afford him some amusement.

Candra lifted her shoulders and dropped them again.

'I'd be a liar if I said it didn't. I really thought I could beat you.' But it had been more than just the race, it was a battle of wills. She had wanted to beat him mentally as well as physically.

'And if I'm perfectly honest,' he replied, 'there was one time when I thought you would win. And that would have hurt me much more than it's hurt you.'

'It's what I planned,' she said sharply.

He looked at her for a moment, then threw back his head and laughed.

Candra smiled, hesitantly at a first, then, unable to help herself, joined in his laughter. Quite how it happened she did not know, but suddenly she was in Simeon's arms, his cool mouth on hers, and an unstoppable sea of desire rushing headlong through her veins.

The kiss went on and on, and she could feel his heart thudding out of control as he must feel hers. It was like being released from the snare which had held her for so long. She had struggled and struggled to keep her feelings at bay, to hide the emotions he was able to create, now there was no halting them. With utter disregard for what he might think, she pressed her body close against his, clinging to him, returning his kisses with a passion that was alien, spiralling in a circle of her own happiness.

'Let's get out of here,' he muttered thickly, his mouth covering her face with hungry kisses.

Candra did not think she had the strength, but she need not have worried. Simeon lifted her into his arms and waded to the steps in the corner, climbing out effortlessly.

On the patio, close to the house, was a swinging

hammock. He carried her to it, then set her down on the floor just in front. Again they came together as though they were two parts of a whole.

Very gently he laid her on the hammock, sitting on the edge himself so that he could look down at her. Not her face, but her body. The rounded curves of her breasts, her slender waist and flat stomach. Awareness and desire built up inside Candra, and she wanted to offer herself to him, so much so that she lifted her arms and hooked them around the back of his neck, pulling him down to her so that they could kiss again.

His kiss was more gentle this time. He cupped her face with his hands, studying it and kissing it with feather-light kisses. 'You're very beautiful, Candra.' His fingers moved down the slender column of her throat, trailing across her shoulders and over the delicate mounds of her breasts.

Candra was totally hypnotised, and when he said, 'Let's dispose of this,' she willingly lifted her body so that he could undo her bikini top.

Although he had seen her naked before, this was different. There had been nothing sexual that first time. Now her whole body ached as his fingers traced her curves, gently at first, rubbing the nubs of his thumbs over her hardened nipples, making her cry out in an agony of pleasure when he took them between thumb and forefinger. It was torture of the most exquisite kind.

But when he lowered his head, and his tongue and teeth replaced his hands, he induced sensations Candra had only half felt in the past. Although at one time she'd thought she was in love with Craig, there had never been anything like this. And Andrew, poor man, left her cold. She realised that now. There was no comparison at all with the feelings raging inside her.

And she did not want to stop, she wanted Simeon to go on kissing her and touching her and inducing these mindless sensations forever. It was as though she had been saving herself just for him .

Then suddenly, abruptly, without warning, he lifted himself away from her. 'I think I've proved my point.'

Candra frowned, not knowing what he was talking about, until suddenly it hit her. This had all been a game. Yesterday she had deliberately resisted him, today she had given it no thought. He had said he would wait his chance, and this had been it. What a blind fool she had been.

She could have cried. The sensations he had created inside her were so potent, so strong, so very, very real. She had been in danger of losing her self-control—while he, damn him, had known exactly what he was doing. He had been playing with her, drawing out a response which must have richly exceeded his expectations. Anger snaked through her with the speed of lightning, and she struck out wildly with her fists. 'You bastard, you sick-minded bastard! How could you do this to me?'

He sprang agilely to his feet and laughed. 'Even though it started out as an experiment, Candra, I can honestly say that it was a very pleasurable experience.'

'I bet it was,' she sneered, pushing herself up also and standing to face him. 'But not pleasurable enough that you couldn't stop when you'd proved your point. Were you comparing me with Briony? I bet you didn't stop halfway through last night.'

'As a matter of fact,' he said, still with that maddening smile on his face, 'I didn't see her.'

'No?' scorned Candra. 'Are you telling me she stood you up?'

'Not exactly, but it's of no importance. I think we should take a shower.'

'Not for me, thank you,' she said with careful politeness. 'I'll have mine on the boat.'

'Running away, Candra?' The gentle taunt had the desired effect. She shrugged and followed him, and stood with closed eyes beneath the ice-cold jets until she felt Simeon's hand on her arm.

With a savage gesture she knocked him away, striding back to the sun loungers and throwing herself down. Her humiliation cut deep. She had given away her innermost feelings and he had rejected them. She felt totally destroyed.

The sun warmed her skin, but did not dispel the chill around her heart, and yet when she looked at Simeon's hard, tanned body stretched out beside her she could still feel the power of his sexuality. Would nothing destroy it? she asked herself achingly. Was she to be forever caged in this prison?

There was another answer. She could marry Andrew. He would be delighted, and she would be protected. But would she be happy? She shook her head as though the question had been asked out loud. Simeon had been right when he'd said she would be bored out of her mind. Andrew could give her none of this mind-shattering excitement. But he could give you peace of mind, urged her conscience. He'll never make demands on you, he'll never try to dominate you. Isn't that what you're trying to escape from?

'There is no escape,' she said.

'From what?' asked Simeon, turning to face her.

Candra frowned, wondering what he was talking about.

'You said there was no escape.'

'Did I? I was thinking, that's all.' Had she really spoken those words aloud?

'What were you thinking'

'Nothing of importance.'

'No?' His eyes widened disbelievingly. 'Perhaps it was me you were thinking about?'

When Candra did not reply, he shrugged dismissively and changed the subject. 'I think it's time we made a move. I don't know about you, but I'm starving.'

'I hope you're not still expecting me to provide lunch?' she asked coldly.

'But of course,' he smiled. 'A bet's a bet.'

He stood up and held out his hand, but Candra ignored it, and as they walked across to *Four Seasons* she did not know how she was going to get through the next hour or so. As always, he would fill the boat with his presence. It was going to be a difficult lunch.

CHAPTER EIGHT

LUNCH was not the ordeal Candra had expected. It had its good moments and its bad, but for the most part Simeon behaved like an amiable big brother, teasing and indulgent, never once hinting that a short time earlier she had been furiously angry with him, and an even shorter time before that they had been locked in a passionate embrace.

She prepared the salad while Candra put chicken portions into the oven and whipped up cream for strawberry pudding. Having been so confident that she would win, Candra had got nothing ready.

'How could you have been so sure?' Simeon wanted to know when she apologised.

'Because I know my own capabilities.'

'But not mine, eh?'

'I thought I did; I was sure I would win.'

'And as I said before, I'm glad you didn't.'

'It might have done you good,' she retorted sharply. 'Men always think they're the superior sex.'

'And aren't we?' There was a twinkle in the brilliant blueness of his eyes, but Candra missed it.

'Not always.' She half wished she had not said that, because he was making a big effort to be friendly and now she was on the verge of destroying it. 'There are a lot of career women today who are as good as any man.'

'That's debatable,' he said. 'Some women are afraid when it comes to taking the last step. They want equality, they want the power, but they're not equipped with the necessary ruthlessness to go with it.'

'You think I'd be too soft?' she demanded.

Simeon nodded. 'I've seen the vulnerable side of you. And there's no room in business for vulnerability.'

I'm only vulnerable where you're concerned, she wanted to say, but knew that would be wrong. 'You'd be surprised how hard I can be when necessary.'

He looked at her quickly. 'I don't think I'd like to see that side of you, Candra.'

She did not ask why. She let the subject drop, opening the oven and checking unnecessarily on the chicken, and when she looked up again he had gone outside with the dogs.

After lunch, to her surprise, he suggested they go out on the boat.

'If you're sure?' she said. She had hoped he would go back to the house. It was hard pretending. She had been deeply hurt by his rejection, and could not understand his ability to act as though nothing had happened. He had been as physically excited as she, even though it had all been a game, so how could he cloak himself now with indifference?

He untied the boat and they set off, Candra steering, Simeon standing by the open doors, the two dogs between them. They were enjoying a late summer this year, and the sun blazed down out of an almost cloudless blue sky. She had changed her swimsuit for a white cotton skirt and a strapless pink top, and Simeon had gone up to the house and pulled on denims and a casual shirt.

For a while neither spoke. Candra tried to concentrate on her steering, but time and time again her eyes were drawn in his direction. She was grateful that he was looking where they were going and had his back to her.

His hair shone blue-black in the sunlight, and Candra fought the temptation to lean forward and touch it. No matter what he had done to her, she still felt this same awareness, this same deep-seated desire to be a part of him.

There was a world of difference between this trip and the one she had taken with Andrew. Her senses had not been heightened then, she had not been aware of every breath Andrew took, she had not felt this insane urge for physical contact. And it was insane, after what he had done to her. His interest lay in Briony; she was a fool to think there could ever be anything between them.

'Look, there's a vole.'

Simeon's voice broke into her thoughts, and she followed the direction of his finger just in time to see the tiny ratlike creature disappear through a hole in the muddy bank.

'How about letting me take over for a while?'

Candra glanced at him sharply. 'Do you know how?'

'But of course,' he answered with an amused smile.

And so reluctantly she gave up the tiller. She guessed he did not very much like her being in charge. He was always in full control of every situation. Just like her father! Without realising it, she compressed her lips, resting her arms on the cabin top and staring straight ahead.

The canal was busy this summer's day, and Simeon hailed other boat people as they passed. There was a togetherness about the situation that Candra had never felt before. She had often taken friends out with her, but this was different. Simeon was too imposing a man to dismiss. She tried and couldn't do it. He was here, and every single second, every fraction of a second even, she was aware of him to the exclusion of all else.

He did not want to form a committed relationship, he had made that perfectly clear, and in all honesty Candra knew that that was not what she wanted either. But one glance, one accidental brush of his body and she went to pieces, and she knew it would only be a matter of time before her reserves dropped away altogether. He could play his games with her and she would be unable to do a thing about it.

The canal passed through Hey, not far from her parents' house. 'Shall we tie up and pay them another visit?' suggested Simeon.

Candra shook her head. 'They won't be at home. They visit my brother and his family on a Sunday.'

'They must be disappointed that you've never married and had children yourself?'

Candra shrugged. 'They've had to accept that my career comes first.'

'And when you've achieved your ambition, when you're actually on the board, what then?'

His eyes were penetrating into the recesses of her mind, and Candra knew nothing less than the truth would satisfy him. But she took so long in thinking about what to say that he answered the question for her.

'Then you'll find that you spend more and more time at the office. Board meetings that run on after everyone else has left, paperwork to be taken home and gone through, business lunches and dinners and trips abroad, and before you know it it will be too late.'

'Too late for what?' She frowned, not altogether liking the picture he had drawn.

'Too late to have babies, perhaps.' A black brow rose.

'Or is it that you don't like children? Don't you intend having any?'

'I think that's my affair,' she said witheringly, though she could not deny that the thought of being made love to by Simeon and bearing his child appealed to her enormously. It also amazed her. She turned abruptly away. 'I'll make a cup of tea.'

His faint smile suggested that he knew exactly what thoughts were going through her mind, but by the time she returned with two mugs of steaming liquid she had squashed her anger. She smiled coolly. 'How far do you intend going?'

'Not fed up yet, are you?' he grinned. 'There's plenty of time.'

They cruised steadily onwards, and each time they came to a lock Candra took over the steering while Simeon did the heavier work of winding the paddles and opening the gates. But always, once they were clear, he took the tiller from her. It was very, very clear that he did not like her being in charge.

It was in Candra's mind to tax him with it, but she did not want to start another argument. She enjoyed these moments they spent together in harmony. They were so infrequent that it was best to savour them while they lasted.

They branched off the Staffordshire and Worcestershire Canal on to the Trent and Mersey, and they stopped in a particularly beautiful stretch where the trees bowed to the water on either side. It was cool, and green and relaxing, and after tying up Simeon suggested a walk.

For almost an hour they strolled, sometimes deviating from the towpath to clamber through the woods, the dogs chasing sticks and discovering scents.

When they got back to the boat they ate ham sandwiches outside on a blanket thrown over the grass. They drank more tea and Candra sliced up a fruit cake.

'You cooked this?' he asked.

She nodded.

'Is there no limit to what you can do?'

'I enjoy cooking,' she said.

'And yet you prefer a lonely career instead of a husband and family?'

Candra groaned inwardly. 'Please don't start that again.'

'Does it offend you?' he asked. 'It shouldn't, not if it's what you truly want out of life.'

'Of course it's what I want,' she snapped. 'Didn't your wife work? Are you against women working?'

She watched the brief shadow that passed over his face. 'No, as a matter of fact, she didn't. As soon as we were married she gave up her job.'

'Was that her choice or yours?'

He frowned. 'You really think I'm that chauvinistic?'

'I don't know,' she answered with a shrug. 'I know you don't approve of what I'm doing.'

'That's different.'

'No, it's not.'

'Yes, it is, Candra. You're missing out on a home, a loving husband, happy children, all the things that mean so much to women, to men too.'

'I'm not just any woman,' she thrust back tersely.

'So I've discovered.' The comment was dry and humourless.

'How long were you married?' Candra decided that she might as well ask all the other questions that had often tumbled through her mind.

'Ten years.'

She had not expected it to be so long, and gave a tiny gasp of surprise. 'I didn't realise. Are you going to marry Briony?' She wondered at her own daring even as she voiced the question.

'Would that trouble you?'

Candra shrugged. 'It's really nothing to do with me, is it? I know it's what Briony has in mind, I simply wondered whether you felt the same.'

'Briony has been a very good friend to me,' he said slowly, 'especially when I needed someone after Marie's death. I owe her a lot.'

In other words, yes, he was going to marry her. Candra felt her face drain of colour, and in that moment knew that she loved Simeon. It had happened without her wanting it or expecting it. Again that feeling of being trapped within her own emotions closed over her. She turned away so that he would not see her agonised expression, and gathered up their plates and cups with trembling hands

She washed up and Simeon brought in the blanket already folded. 'I think we should make a move.' He seemed not to notice her change of mood.

Candra glanced at her watch. It was a minute to seven. It would be almost dark when they got home. She had never expected, when Simeon had suggested a boat ride, that they would stay out this long. Altogether she had been in his company seven hours, the longest stretch of time they had ever spent together. It hadn't seemed that long, and she surprised herself by admitting how much she had enjoyed it. She wished now that she hadn't asked about Briony.

He turned the key and pressed the starter button, and the engine pulsed into life. They were still heading away from home as it was too narrow to turn here, and Candra was not sure how far they needed to go before finding a winding hole.

In fact they travelled a further half-hour. Candra watched Simeon manoeuvre the boat and was forced to admire his skill. Narrow-boats were not easy things to turn, but he handled it as though he had been doing it all his life.

They were in almost exactly the same spot where they had picnicked when, for no obvious reason, the engine petered out.

'Fuel?' asked Simeon with a frown, glancing at the gauge.

'It doesn't work,' she said, 'but I don't think so.'

'You don't *think* so?' The frown gouged even deeper.

'I know it isn't,' she answered, trying to sound confident, but not altogether sure.

'Has it done this sort of thing before?'

'Never.'

'We'd better tie up and take a look.'

The engine was housed beneath the stern deck. Simeon lifted the cover and stepped down into the engine hole. Candra watched helplessly as he methodically inspected. She hoped that whatever was wrong he would be able to put it right.

'There's no diesel getting through,' he said at length. 'There must be a blockage somewhere.' He spent several more minutes testing before hauling himself out. 'How do you check your fuel?'

'With a dipstick.'

He took the cap off her fuel tank and put in the stick

which Candra silently handed to him. It came out empty. His look said it all. 'You have a spare can for emergencies?'

Candra shook her head. She felt a complete and utter fool, and wished she could slide into the water and melt away. Why, oh, why hadn't she checked the fuel recently?

'You do realise that we're in the middle of nowhere?' His voice whipped across the space between them, making Candra flinch as though she had been struck.

'I know.' Her response was scarcely more than a whisper.

'Heaven knows where the nearest filling station is.' Blue eyes blazed angrily into hers. 'But I do know one thing, Candra Drake, and that is that I'm not chasing around at this hour. We'll sleep on the boat and sort things out tomorrow.'

Alarm filtered through her. 'But——'

'But nothing,' he cut in shortly. 'For an intelligent woman, you've been remarkably stupid. When was the last time you filled up?'

'Months ago,' admitted Candra reluctantly. 'I never go far. The fuel seems to last forever.'

'And it's my bad luck that it chose this moment to run out,' he snorted. 'You do realise that this diesel engine has to be bled once it runs dry? It's not a simple matter of just filling up and going.'

'I'm sorry,' she muttered. She had never felt so incredibly foolish in her life. He was right to be angry with her.

'And so you damn well should be,' he snarled.

He washed and dried his hands, and threw himself down on one of the seats. Candra could see what sort of a night it was going to be.

'Would you like a drink?' she asked tentatively.

'A Scotch? Yes. Thank you.'

She poured out a measure and handed it to him. He swallowed half and put the glass down.

'Are you hungry? Shall I make us some supper?' Candra prided herself on being in complete control of any situation. Now she had made such an idiot of herself that she was unable to think straight.

'No, thanks.'

'Perhaps we could stop a passing boat and ask them to fetch us some diesel, or even tow us to the nearest boatyard?' she suggested hopefully.

'Which is at least eight miles away,' he snapped. 'In any case, they'd be closed. We'll wait till morning, then find a filling station. There's sure to be one nearer than the boat yard.'

Candra could tell by the tone of his voice that he wasn't happy about staying here. And nor was she. It looked like being one hell of an unpleasant experience. She went into the kitchen and made herself a cup of coffee, taking as long over it as she could before joining him in the lounge area.

His eyes were closed, though Candra felt sure he was not asleep. She picked up a magazine and leafed through it, and the next time she ventured a glance at him he was watching her.

'I truly am sorry,' she said softly.

'As well you should be,' he growled. 'I'm disappointed in you, Candra.'

She grimaced. 'I'm disappointed in myself.'

'What would your father say, I wonder?' This time there was a hint of a smile as he spoke.

'I dare not think. He hates incompetence.'

'I shall need some persuading not to tell him.' A definite smile now softened his face.

'Such as what?'

'Supper, for a start. I've decided I am hungry after all.'

Candra wasn't sure whether she wanted to know what else he had in mind, so she sprang to her feet. 'How about lasagne?'

'Sounds good.'

'It's frozen, but it won't take long.'

After popping it into the oven, she prepared a tossed green salad and laid the table. When there was nothing else left to do she rejoined Simeon. He was glancing through her magazine and she watched him unobserved.

How ironic that after all her vows never to fall in love again she had done so with a man who was the breed she hated most. And, what was more humiliating, he had no feelings for her. He was going to marry someone else!

She ached to be held in his arms, to be crushed against his hard chest, to feel his mouth on hers. Even thinking about it set her pulses clamouring, and she did not even realise that he had put down the magazine and was watching her.

'If I didn't know better, I'd think you were after my body.'

Candra laughed away her nervousness, appalled to discover that he had caught her looking at him. She had held nothing back; everything she felt was in her eyes.

'Then it's a good job you do know better,' she retorted, embarrassment making her tone sharp.

'It's a pity. It's going to be a long evening, and an

even longer night.'

Candra's eyes widened. 'I hope you're not suggesting what I think you're suggesting?' Her heart skittered at the very thought.

'And what would that be?' There was a wicked smile on his face now. He had completely got over his earlier anger.

'I don't have to put it into words,' she said, attempting to be cross with him, but failing. Getting through the next twelve or so hours without giving herself away was going to be one of the hardest things she had ever had to do. 'I think I'll go and check the oven.'

But as she stood up he caught her wrist. 'Running away again, Candra? Why don't you relax? I can assure you I don't bite.'

It was as though he had plugged her into an electric socket. She could feel shock-waves running along her arm and through her body, and she had a quick mental image of herself lighting up like a neon tube.

He pulled her down on to his lap and her longing for him pounded through her veins. But still she protested. 'No, Simeon, no.' She flattened her hand against his chest, intending to push herself free, and felt the hammer-beat of his heart. If she did not escape now it would be too late.

But his arms tightened. 'Don't fight the inevitable.' His words were no more than a warm breath across her face, and when his mouth claimed hers wave after wave of hunger and need shuddered through her. How could she deny herself this pleasure when it had been so long since any other man had touched her, when he had been awakening dormant senses from the very first moment they'd met?

None of it made any sense, but it had happened, so why not accept it? Why not let this man love her a little? Their tongues touched, an impossible heat invaded her, and every atom of resolve melted.

How long the kiss lasted she did not know. It could have been minutes, it could have been seconds, it could even have been hours, but it seemed disappointingly brief. 'I think,' he said softly, 'that I can smell something burning.'

With a cry Candra raced to the kitchen. The lasagne was crispy brown, but not uneatable. She opened a bottle of wine and paused a moment before lighting the candles she had already placed on the table. What would Simeon think? It was not a romantic ploy—she often used them when sitting listening to music or watching television—but after what had just happened would he think it was deliberate?

When his hands touched her shoulders it was too late to do anything about it. 'Allow me,' he said, taking the matches from her and lighting the candles. They sat down and he poured the wine and helped her to the lasagne. The green salad was a particular favourite of Candra's, made from lettuce and cucumber, small seedless green grapes and green pepper, apple and celery, all tossed in a sweet dressing.

'This is really delicious,' he complimented. 'Almost worth running out of fuel for.'

They ate their meal in relative silence, his eyes on her often, and when they had finished he surprised her by offering to wash up. It was something her father never did, nor Craig. They both said it was a woman's job. She had expected Simeon to be of the same mind.

Afterwards they took the dogs for a walk. A full moon

turned night into day and the water into molten silver.
The black silhouette of a lone duck sailed silently by. It
was magical.

He took her hand into his and they spoke softly, afraid
that loud words would shatter the stark beauty. Once
Simeon stilled her, and on the other side of the canal she
saw a fox creeping along the towpath.

They heard night sounds. The far-off hoot of an owl,
the rustling of tiny creatures in the long grass, the plop
of a fish or a vole, but loudest of all was Candra's heart.

An inner excitement filled her and overflowed,
anticipation, expectation. She was conscious only of
Simeon and the hours that lay ahead. Their need of each
other. She dared not ask herself why he should need her
when he had Briony. She forced Briony from her mind.
This was now, herself and Simeon, two people who felt
a mutual hunger.

The first thing they did when they got back was make
up Simeon's bed. The dining-table dropped down to
form the base, and the seats became his mattress.
Candra reached sheets and a duvet from the storage
space beneath the seats, and in no time at all it was ready.
She could not help thinking that it was big enough for
the two of then, and was acutely disappointed when
Simeon made no further attempt to touch her.

'How about a hot chocolate before I turn in?' he
asked.

Always he surprised her. Hot chocolate instead of a
whisky nightcap. It didn't sound like him at all.
Carefully she measured milk into a saucepan and
brought it to the boil, pouring it over the chocolate
powder which she had spooned into two mugs. After
stirring them, she handed one to Simeon and took the

other herself. Their eyes met, and he groaned and put down his mug. 'It's no good, I can't fight it any longer.' He took her mug too and pulled her unresisting body hard against him.

Candra stood there, melting, and for a few seconds he merely held her, stroking her hair, allowing his strength to flood into her and her sweetness into him.

'Candra. Candra.' He murmured her name over and over again, edging her slowly out of the kitchen and into the dining-room. They sat down on the edge of his bed, and Simeon turned her to him holding her face between his palms, looking at her deeply. 'I don't know what it is you do to me, but I can't help myself.'

He traced every inch of her face with gentle fingertips. He touched her mouth and pulled down her lower lip, kissing the moist softness inside. He kissed the tip of her nose and her eyelids and her ears and her throat, and Candra felt as though she were spinning in space. She pressed her soft, womanly body into the hardness of his. Everything inside her danced and burned, feelings welled and spilled.

Reaching up, she touched his face too, feeling the hard angles and the day's growth of beard, and his thick black brows, and his sculptured lips. He took her fingers into his mouth and kissed them, then his hands slid slowly down over the gentle curve of her breasts.

Candra groaned as a wild, impossible heat invaded her. Her breasts welled and hardened, and she arched herself into him, threading her fingers through the silky wiriness of his hair, her lips parted, her eyes half closed, her mind spiralling somewhere out in space. His touch was so light, and yet it sent explosions of feeling shattering through her.

With one swift movement he dispensed of her top, revealing the silken nakedness of her aching breasts. She fell back against the pillow, and his fingers teased and tormented and his lips followed, and she gasped when first one nipple and then the other was sucked into the heated moistness of his mouth.

Her fingers clutched his shoulders, nails digging, her whole body a mass of uncontrollable sensation. She frantically tore away his shirt, buttons popping, finally feeling the freedom of his flesh. Smooth, hard, warm, damp.

Not once did she stop to think that what she was doing was wrong. Not once did she think of Briony. She was beyond coherent thought. Her head, her mind, her body were no longer her own. They belonged to Simeon.

His hand moved down over her stomach, his kisses followed in a burning trail of destruction. Her body ached as her skirt was removed. She trembled and shuddered as he stroked and kissed and explored. No part of her was kept secret from this man.

It was not until he slid out of his jeans and she was pulled against him, it was not until there was no mistaking his intention, that a thread of sanity crept in. She had not expected him to take things this far. She couldn't do it. It was too big a step to take when there was no future in it. No other man had ever taken her, and she couldn't let Simeon. Not when he was going to marry Briony!

She had been transported to a world where only senses mattered, where insane things were sane and the two of them were one. But now it was time to come back to earth, to part, to restore normality.

'Simeon.' Her hand on his shoulder checked him. He

instantly sensed that there was something different about her touch. 'Simeon, I can't go on.' Her voice was a bare whisper.

Whatever he had expected, it was not that. He drew in a ragged breath and glazed eyes tried to focus. His frown asked her why.

'It's all wrong, I should never have. . .' How could she go on after the encouragement she had given him? Her fingers curled into her palms, her arms crossed over her breasts, and she drew up her knees and huddled miserably away from him.

She expected anger, she expected him to force himself on her, and was stunned when he sprang away and without a word began to get dressed.

'Simeon, I'm sorry. It was wrong of me to let you think that——'

He turned around and she recoiled at the blazing ice in his eyes. 'Don't bother apologising. I should have known you hadn't the guts to carry it through. I'm amazed you let me get as far as I did. What went wrong, did you forget to put your shutters up?'

Candra grimaced her pain. 'No! No, Simeon. I wanted to go on, but sex for the sake of sex—I can't do it.'

'Of course, sex for the sake of sex,' he growled. 'I should have known that's all it was to you.'

And you, she wanted to cry, but didn't. What was the point in arguing? What was done was done. Once they got home Briony would satisfy his needs and she would be left to sleep alone.

She dragged herself off the bed, gathered up her clothes, and dazedly made her way through to her own bedroom. She shut the folding doors, but there was nothing to keep him out should he decide to come and take what she had denied him.

CHAPTER NINE

CANDRA pulled on her nightdress. It was all going wrong. She did not want any other man in her life; she did not even want an affair. Yet when Simeon was near she could not help herself. One look out of those sensual blue eyes and she was helpless, one touch of those strong brown fingers and she was out of control.

How could this happen to her? How could this one man change views she had held for years? It did not make sense. Nothing made sense any more. She could actually still feel his hands and his mouth on her, burning her skin, arousing feelings she had been ignorant of.

Looking at her reflection in the mirror, Candra saw a stranger. A woman with softly parted lips, with glowing skin, and eyes that told of complete arousal. They hid nothing, none of the aching need, none of her love, none of her passion. She stood looking for several long seconds, touching her cheeks and her lips with trembling fingertips. She was beautiful, a completely different person—and Simeon had done this to her!

She wanted to scream out with the injustice of it all. She didn't want to love him, she didn't want to feel like this. She wanted to carry on with her life the way it had been before she met him. It had been orderly and safe, and there were none of these uncertainties, and she wanted it back that way.

Her shoulders sagged as she turned from the mirror, and she gave an inward groan because she needed to use the bathroom. She did not want to face Simeon again tonight. She felt too vulnerable. She had given too much of herself to him.

She pulled on her wrap and opened the door cautiously. If luck was with her he would have gone to bed, and she could get in and out of the bathroom without him seeing her. But luck was not with her. Simeon sat on the edge of his bed, still wearing his jeans, his mug of chocolate cradled in his hands.

Candra flinched all over again at the coldness in his eyes, but he said nothing, and she told herself that she was glad. It was best this affair ended before it went any further. She washed her hands and face and, when she was finished, opened the door, intending to slip back to her room without looking at him.

Instead he was standing outside, arms folded across his magnificently muscled chest. 'Just for the record, Candra,' he said coolly, 'I am not in the habit of making love just for the sheer hell of it. I happen to find you a very attractive woman.'

She swallowed hard and glared. 'So that makes a difference, does it? That gives you the right to make love to me?'

His eyes narrowed. 'You wanted it as much as I did.'

'Until I came to my senses,' she snapped. 'I have to admit, Simeon, that you're a very difficult man to resist. But I'm glad that I did. At least I'll be able to sleep with a clear conscience. Excuse me.'

He let her go without a word, much to her surprise, but as she slid beneath her quilt Candra knew that sleep would be impossible. He had made sure of that. It was wrong, though, to lay all the blame on Simeon. She had been as eager as he to make love, and she could not help wondering whether she would be lying here alone if she had let things reach their natural conclusion. She doubted it very much. They would almost certainly have remained locked in each other's arms until morning.

She turned on to her back, her legs outstretched, her hands beneath her head, and listened as he moved about the boat—washing the mugs, going to the bathroom, unzipping his jeans, the rustle as he pulled them off. Would he sleep in his underpants, or would he take them off too? She had a swift mental picture of his strong, naked body, and hot desire pulsed through her. But eventually all became still.

If she hadn't ran out of diesel this would never have happened, she told herself. Simeon would never have discovered how easily she responded to him. All she could be grateful for was that he did not know the full extent of her feelings. What a fool to fall in love when she had her whole life planned. And how difficult it was going to be to push him out of her mind. No, not difficult, *impossible*. How could you forget that you loved someone?

Candra curled on her side and tried to sleep, but she tossed and turned the hours away, and in the end decided that a hot milk drink was the only solution. She got out of bed and pulled on her wrap, silently letting herself out of the cabin. Skye opened a lazy eye and looked at her; Lady slept on.

She paused on her way to the kitchen to look at the sleeping Simeon. A stray moonbeam lit his pillow and she had a crazy urge to touch him. How could he sleep after all that had happened? Didn't it mean anything to him? Didn't he feel this same stirring of the senses that defied all reason?

With reluctance, she dragged herself away, opening the fridge and taking out a bottle of milk. Her eyes were accustomed to the darkness and she needed no light, but the cupboard door creaked as she slid it open and the saucepan clinked on another. She held her breath and hoped she had not woken him. Once the milk was in the saucepan and on the stove, all that could be heard was the faint hiss of the gas beneath it.

Candra stood and watched the blue flames licking round the sides of the pan. She thought of Simeon's tongue licking her breasts and she felt a fresh ache in her groin. She closed her eyes and let the feelings flood through her, and the next second heard a sizzle as the milk boiled up and frothed over.

'Oh, damn!' she whispered fiercely, turning off the gas. Now she would have to switch on the light, and she hadn't wanted to do that.

But even as the light flickered Simeon appeared at her side, naked except for brief red and black underpants. Every nerve responded and she wanted to forget the milk, she wanted to forget everything except him. She wanted to be held once more against him, to feel the strong beat of his heart, to inhale the earthy male smell of him.

'What's going on?' he asked gruffly. 'Can't you sleep?'

Candra struggled to compose herself and her tone was deliberately sharp. 'I see you had no such trouble.'

'I've never suffered from conscience,' he admitted.

'I can believe that,' she said. 'You'd never have carried on with your development if you did.' She reached a cloth and began mopping up the burnt milk, and wished it didn't have to be this way.

'I wondered when we'd get round to that again.'

Candra missed the narrowing of his eyes, but she heard the aggression in his tone. 'It's what began all this, isn't it? I wish to heaven I'd never met you.'

'And I sometimes wish that I'd never met you.'

'Only sometimes?' she jeered.

'You're the most infuriating female I've ever come across.'

'And you, as a matter of fact are the most infuriating man I've ever met,' she flung back. And the most sexy, and the most attractive, and the only one to have ever affected her like this. She washed the saucepan and put it away. There was no point in heating more milk. Nothing in the world would make her sleep now.

'Were your thoughts so far away that you let the milk boil over?'

'I imagine you know the answer to that,' she said drily. 'I'm sorry if I disturbed you. I'll go back to bed now so that you can get on with your sleep.'

'Do you know,' he said slowly, 'I have the strangest feeling that I won't sleep any more. Let's sit together for a while.'

Candra looked at him in alarm. Did he realise what he was asking of her?

He snorted angrily. 'I promise not to touch you. In fact, I promise not to touch you ever again. You made your point very clear. The next move, if there is one, will have to come from you.'

Candra's muscles curled up tight inside as she moved through into the lounge. She ought to be glad, but she wasn't. It would be hell seeing Simeon but not feeling the touch of his hand or his lips brushing over hers.

He sat in one corner of the settee, she in the other, her

feet curled beneath her. They talked quietly about anything and everything, and gradually Candra relaxed, her eyelids grey heavy, and she slept.

When she awoke she was in her own bed and it was daylight. She still felt the sexual excitement Simeon had stimulated. It was a wonderful, wonderful feeling. She stretched and smiled and the sun filtered through her curtains. It felt good to be alive. And then she remembered.

A frown replaced her smile. This was not where she had gone to sleep. She had rowed with Simeon; she had rejected him. He must have put her to bed. He had taken off her wrap and her slippers, and he had drawn the quilt over her—and all after his promise not to touch her again! Her cheeks flamed at the thought of being held against that hard body, and she could not help wondering whether he had done anything else. Whether he had kissed her mouth, or let his hand graze her breasts. They peaked and hardened at the very thought. It was a strange feeling that he had held her close while she knew nothing about it.

Was he awake yet? Was he lying there thinking about her? She smiled faintly, and at that moment he banged on her door. 'If we're to get anywhere today you'd better get up.'

His brusque voice dispelled all happy thoughts. So much for her daydreams. He had probably ripped off her wrap and tossed her mercilessly into bed. 'I'm awake,' she called. 'I'll be out in a minute.'

She hurried to the bathroom and he was nowhere in sight. She got dressed and discovered tea and toast on the dining-room table. There was no sign at all that he had slept there last night. But she would never forget it.

She could see in her mind's eye his dark head on the pillow and the shape of him beneath the quilt, knees drawn up slightly because the bed wasn't long enough for him to stretch out.

She poured herself a cup of tea and was nibbling on a square of toast when he came in. He looked fresh and bright-eyed, and the stubble on his chin was quite attractive. 'Thank you for this,' she said. 'You didn't have to.'

'I was beginning to think you would never wake.'

She frowned. 'What time is it?' Her alarm clock had stopped and she hadn't yet put on her watch.

'Almost nine.'

Candra's mouth fell open. 'And you let me lie in! Good lord, I must ring the office, and we need diesel, and——'

He silenced her with a glance. 'Don't panic. It's all in hand.'

She frowned. 'What do you mean?'

'I've already fetched diesel, and I left a message on your company's answering machine that you were taking the day off.'

'You've what?' gasped Candra. 'I can't do that. I've got too much to do.'

'It will wait. It will take us a good half-day to get home, and by the time we've stopped for lunch it will be well into the afternoon.'

She glared her resentment. 'Why do you insist on organising my life?'

'You haven't proved to me that you're capable of doing it yourself. Eat your toast.'

She decided to ignore the jibe. 'Aren't you having any?'

'I've already eaten.'

'And the dogs, how about them?'

'Skye came with me to the garage. Lady had a good run while I was working.'

'What time were you up?' she frowned.

'About six.'

'Then you've had hardly any sleep.'

'As if that would worry you,' he commented drily. 'Come on, eat up.'

When she had finished Candra went up on to the stern deck. 'Are you ready?' he asked. 'Shall we move?'

Candra nodded, and wished there weren't this barrier between them. He was perfectly polite, but that rapport of yesterday was missing. And it was all her own fault. Though she did not regret what she had done. It would have been a bitter memory once he was married to Briony.

She untied one rope while he did the other. The stakes were fetched out and stored neatly away. The engine, after only the slightest hesitation, sprang into life. He went much more slowly than the four-miles-per-hour speed limit, seeming in no hurry at all to get home, and Candra raised no objection. This was likely to be the very last time they went out together.

She disappeared below and washed up the breakfast things, and when they eventually reached the boatyard Simeon refused to let her pay for the diesel. 'But you can't keep paying for everything,' she demurred. 'First my car, now this.'

'You're the first woman I've ever met who's complained.'

Her chin lifted. 'I'm probably the first one to stop you making love as well. I'm sorry, but that's the way I am.

I have very strong principles.'

'So I'm beginning to realise.'

Candra anticipated a difficult journey home, with Simeon concentrating entirely on steering *Four Seasons* and ignoring her. She could not have been more wrong. They chatted and laughed, and his eyes were on her often, warming her skin, making her sick with wanting him, and she could not explain why he had this power.

They tied up at a canal-side pub for a roast beef lunch, and their knees almost touched under the table. Almost, but not quite. Simeon adhered strictly to the rules he had made. Not once did he touch her, deliberately or accidentally, but he made very sure that she knew how he felt. It was a planned assault on her senses, and during the afternoon Candra came very close to flinging herself into his arms. How she stopped herself she did not know.

It was a relief when they arrived home. They tied up the boat and he looked at her and said, 'It's been a very—illuminating trip, Candra. I'll see you tomorrow evening, perhaps?'

'I don't think it would be wise,' she said at once.

One black brow quirked. 'Why is that?'

'Because—because—oh, you know why.'

'Do I?'

'Yes, you damn well do. Now go, just go.'

He smiled easily. 'I intend winning, Candra. I haven't met you just to let you go. One day, and one day soon you'll be in my arms again. You'll be mine, and there won't be a thing you can do about it.'

He turned and strode away before she could speak, but Candra knew he was right. If he continued seeing her, if he continued to wear down her defences, she would lose her control and become his lover. Her throat ached at the mere thought, but she knew it was no answer. Once she had let him into her heart, into her mind, he would begin to take over. She would suddenly find that she was not her own woman after all. She could not do it. She had been hurt too much in the past to let it happen again.

The next day Simeon phoned her at the office, and she could not imagine what he wanted. Nor could she stop the tingle of excitement that ran through her at the sound of his voice.

'Candra, I have to go to New York for a few days. I thought I should tell you so that you won't worry about me.'

The mocking confidence in his tone irritated her. He knew her too well. 'Why should I do that?' she demanded bluntly. 'It will be a relief knowing that I shan't have to lock my doors.'

She heard the soft whistle of his anger and immediately regretted her words. 'I'm sorry,' she said, 'that was uncalled for.'

'But it was obviously in your thoughts,' he grated. 'If I'm really that much of a nuisance, then say so.'

'You're not,' she admitted. 'I simply resented the fact that you know me so well. I would have worried. Thank you for letting me know.'

He grunted something unintelligible and put down the phone, and Candra was left feeling embarrassed. He'd had the courtesy to phone her and she'd been rude. She couldn't imagine what had made her say what she had. Simeon had his faults, but forcing himself on her was not one of them.

She felt miserable for the rest of the morning, and

when, just after lunch, her secretary rang through saying that a Miss Briony Hall wanted to see her she groaned her disbelief. 'Tell her I'm out.' Briony was the last person she wanted to see.

'I'm sorry,' said the girl anxiously, 'she already knows you're in. She said she was a friend of yours.'

Candra sighed. 'Very well. But tell her I can't spare more than a couple of minutes.'

Briony was wearing a cream silk suit and a smile of malicious pleasure. She walked straight across to Candra's desk and placed her hands on it, leaning forward to look into her face. 'I suppose you thought you were very clever, running out of diesel and forcing Simeon to stay the night with you?' Her violet eyes narrowed and became evil. 'But treasure the memory, because it's the last you'll see of him. We're leaving for New York in just over an hour, and when we come back, if we come back, we'll be married.'

Candra gasped.

'I've surprised you, have I?' sneered Briony. 'I thought I would. You're foolish to have read anything into what Simeon did, because he was simply having a last fling. It's natural in a man as sexually motivated as he is, but once we're married he'll never stray, I can assure you of that.'

'If that's all you've come to say then I suggest you leave.' Candra's tone was cool, nothing in her face giving away how much she was hurt. She would not degrade herself by bandying words

Briony pushed herself up, still with that infuriating smile on her painted lips. 'With pleasure. And, if you know what's good for you, you'll move yourself and your boat before we come back from our honeymoon.'

Not until Briony had left the room did Candra realise that she was holding her breath, and with release her whole body threatened to collapse. If what Briony said was true, and she had no reason to think the girl was lying, why hadn't Simeon told her? She had assumed he was going to New York alone, that it was business that took him there. What the hell kind of a monster was he, that he could make love to one girl one day and marry another the next?

Her anger grew, the more she thought about it. She had known that one day he would marry Briony, but not this soon. Her head began to ache, and it was impossible to concentrate. She picked up her bag, leaving her desk exactly as it was, telling her surprised secretary that she was taking the rest of the day off.

She dared not go back to the boat, not yet. There was every chance that Simeon would be in the house, and she did not want to see him. She would not be able to hold her tongue. He must have known all the weekend that he was going to New York, that he was going to get married, and yet it hadn't stopped him wanting to make love to her. The thought was galling.

She left her car and walked, walked blindly, not caring where she went, but not surprised when she found herself near her old moorings. Until she met Simeon this had been a haven, a retreat, a place where the world could pass her by.

But Candra found no solace now. She expected to find Simeon's marina well under construction. Instead the canal basin had not been touched. The warehouses were assuming a completely new appearance, and excavations for the marina had taken place the other side of the wall, but that was as far as it went. Candra could not believe her eyes. *He had tricked her!* He had tricked her into moving!

Her anger deepened to a burning red rage, and she knew now that she had to see him before he left. He was not going to get away with this. She tried his office first, just in case, but was told that he was away for the week on business. The house was empty too. She banged and banged on the door without any response, peering in windows, calling his name, but it was no good. He was not there. She was to late. He had gone.

She sat on her boat and fumed, and day followed day in a kind of haze. Her actions became purely automatic. She dictated letters and attended meetings, but her mind was elsewhere. All she could think about was Simeon and Briony, Briony and Simeon. Simeon married. Simeon making love to Briony. It hurt, it hurt damnably, and yet it shouldn't have. She did not want him, she did not want any man, so why the hell couldn't she cast away the love she felt for him and write it off as a bad experience?

Never had a week been so long, and each day she watched out for their return. It was unwise staying here, she knew that, but something inside would not let her move until she had seen Simeon one last time. The only way she could get him out of her system was by having a blazing row—and seeing him actually married to Briony!

Saturday came and went and they still had not returned and on Sunday afternoon Andrew came to see her. Ever since their last meeting he had carefully avoided her, and she was surprised to see him now. 'I heard from a friend that Simeon was away,' he explained. 'I thought you might like some company.

Candra wondered whether Andrew knew Simeon was honeymooning, or whether he was of the same opinion as everyone else. 'I suppose I am a bit lonely,' she said, which was the understatement of the year. She felt as desolate as hell. 'Come on in and I'll make you a cup of tea.'

'When's he coming back?'

'I've no idea.'

He frowned at the sharpness of her tone. 'He hasn't told you?'

Candra shook her head. 'There's no reason why he should.'

'But I thought that you and he were pretty close these days?'

She picked up the kettle and turned to the sink. 'We've never been that close.'

Andrew grasped her shoulders and spun her to face him. 'But there's something wrong, isn't there? You've been going round the office like a zombie all week, and you look like death warmed up. Are you ill, or is it that swine? What has he done to you?'

Candra shrugged out of his grasp. 'I'd rather not talk about it.'

'Have you fallen out with him?'

'I suppose you could say that.'

'Either you have or you haven't.' Andrew grew irritated by her reluctance to discuss Simeon.

'There's another woman in his life.' She could not bring herself to say that he had actually got married.

'Is that all?' He visibly relaxed. 'Heavens, Candra, I thought it was far worse than that. I thought he'd got you pregnant and then dumped you or something. In any case, I never thought he was right for you. You'll soon get over him.'

She nodded and went back to filling the kettle. Andrew hadn't the slightest idea how deeply she was hurt.

'I think it might be a good idea if you moved away from here,' he said.

She shrugged. 'I suppose so.'

'You could always sell the boat and buy a house.'

'No.' She moved away from the sink and reached out two mugs. 'I don't want to do that. It's cheap, it's easy to keep clean, it's perfect.'

'We'll go looking for fresh moorings together, then. How about right now?'

'I don't think so, Andrew.' She smiled to soften her words. 'I'm not in the mood.'

'Tomorrow night, then?'

'We'll see.'

She made the tea and they drank it, and afterwards took the dogs for a walk. He tried to pump her about Simeon, but she was saying nothing, and when they got back to the boat he accepted her invitation to stay to tea. She wished he hadn't. She had made the offer out of politeness, but would have preffered to be alone.

When finally he went she accompanied him to his car—and Simeon's BMW was standing next to it! 'He's back,' said Andrew needlessly.

Candra's heart skittered. *They* were back. The lovebirds! She felt sick, her head began to swim, and in case Simeon was watching her through the window she flung her arms around Andrew and gave him an enthusiastic goodbye kiss. Get a load of this, Simeon Sterne, she said to herself. Andrew looked surprised but pleased, and had no idea that it was an act of self-preservation.

She watched him go, all the time deliberating whether to march up to the front door and tax Simeon about the marina, or wait until she could get him on his own. Perhaps the latter might be best. It would be difficult speaking to him with the beautiful Briony hanging on his arm.

In the event, she did not have to seek Simeon out—he came to see her. She had been back on *Four Seasons* for almost an hour, fuelling her rage, building it up into a white-hot fury out of all proportion. The marina development was serving as an excuse to hide her real anger over his marriage.

The boat rocked as he stepped on board, and he called out her name at the same time. Candra shot to her feet, and her eyes blazed green as she invited him down.

He wore black trousers and a black shirt, and the dogs launched themselves ecstatically at him, but his smile was wiped cleanly off his face when he saw Candra's hostile expression. His steps slowed and he approached her warily. 'Do I take it I'm not welcome?'

'I think you should know the answer to that,' she slammed, damning her traitorous heart for beating so wildly at the mere sight of him. He looked so fit and well, and why shouldn't he when he had just returned from honeymoon?

'Has this anything to do with what happened last weekend?'

He moved closer to her and Candra edged backwards. The smell of his maleness was powerfully primitive, and it threatened her sanity. She had not intended this meeting to take place on the boat. It was too confined. There was no room to run. He filled it with his dangerous presence.

'Have you been sitting brooding while I've been away, and decided that you'd prefer to put an end to our relationship? Is that it? Have you chosen the coward's way out, Candra?'

Her delicate brows arched scornfully. 'Did you leave me any choice?'

He frowned. 'This is a free world. Everyone has a choice.'

'Of course.' She had the choice whether to conduct an affair with a married man or shut him out of her life altogether. She had to admit she was surprised he still wanted to carry on seeing her, but it proved she had been right all along to distrust him. Were there no men at all in the world who could give a woman what she wanted? Love, loyalty, trust, consideration.

It had been bad enough that he'd wanted to make love to her before he got married, but to want to carry on seeing her now was too appalling for words. Did Briony know what type of a man he was?'

'You say that, Candra, as though you don't mean it.'

'Of course I damn well don't mean it!' she yelled. 'You forced me into this situation, Simeon. And for that I hate you. '

'Suppose you tell me exactly what you think this situation is?'

His eyes were steady on hers, and Candra could not look at him. All the time her heart was banging, her pulses racing, and she felt like flinging herself at him and taking all he had to offer, and to hell with everything else. But she thought about Briony, and she thought about his trickery over the marina, and her anger spurted back into life. 'Let's start with Briony.' She hadn't meant to say that, she hadn't wanted to mention his marriage, but it was done now and there was nothing she could do about it.

'Ah!'

Did that mean he was expecting this confrontation? Had Briony told him that she'd been to see her? She swallowed hard and looked at him bravely. 'She's well, I hope?' There was no mistaking the acid sweetness in her tone.

'Briony's always well. She's one of those disgustingly healthy girls. How nice of you to ask about her. Perhaps I should enquire the same of Andrew? It was he whom I saw leaving a short time ago?'

'If you saw him, then you know,' she retorted sharply.

'How many other times has he been here while I was away?' There was an edge of hardness to his tone now, and his narrowed eyes watched her face carefully. 'Every night?'

'I can't see why it should make any difference to you.'

'It makes a hell of a difference if you're allowing him into your bed,' he snarled. 'Have you any idea at all how much your rejection hurt me?'

'It's no more than you deserve,' she snapped.

A frown gouged his brow. 'And what is that supposed to mean?'

Was he being deliberately obtuse? Or did he enjoy tormenting her like this? She was still fighting the urge to touch him, to close her body up to his and feel his masculine hardness and his strength. Her only defence was anger. 'It means that I think your attitude stinks. No self-respecting man would play around with another girl when he was on the verge of getting married.'

His blue eyes widened. 'So that's why you stopped me? Why the hell didn't you say so, instead of going on about principles? I could have told you that——'

'Would it have made any difference?' she cut in angrily. 'I don't think so. I don't think you give a damn about my feelings. You're all self, the same as every other man. Let's get off the subject of Briony for the moment and on to the real issue.'

'Which is?' His blue eyes grew icy. The warmth that had been in them when he arrived disappeared.

'The marina.'

Thick brows rose, and he waited.

'You lied to me.'

'Did I?'

'You know damn well you did.' She shook her head, his stillness fuelling her anger. Her heavy corn-gold hair brushed the sides of her face, and she knocked it away impatiently. 'You tricked me, Simeon. You told me you were starting work on the basin when you weren't.'

'Perhaps we hit a snag?'

'Perhaps pigs might fly,' she scorned. 'You can try to fob me off with all the excuses under the sun, but I shan't believe you. I believe only what my eyes tell me.'

'Then you're a fool.'

'Not any more. You duped me good and proper, I'll admit that, but now I know where I stand, and you'd be doing both yourself and me a favour if you got out of here now and I never saw you again.'

He looked at her for an endless moment, eyes narrowed but not quite hiding blazing blue depths, a tell-tale muscle jerking spasmodically in his jaw. 'It would be a pity, Candra, to end everything just because of a misunderstanding.'

'Misunderstanding?' she shouted. 'Downright lies, I would call it. I don't know how you have the nerve to——'

Her words were silenced by his hands coming down on her shoulders, a none too gentle finger on her lips. 'Candra, I have never knowingly lied to you.'

Her eyes scorned him. 'You expect me to believe that?'

'I don't expect you to, I want you to.'

She snapped her eyes shut. 'Go to hell.'

His fingers bit into her soft flesh. 'Look at me, damn you. The marina project was stopped because of seepage problems.'

'And you didn't think it important enough to tell me?'

'I forget about work when I'm with you.'

'Spare me the blarney,' she protested, wondering how she would fill the void in her life when he left. Even now she could feel him flowing into her. It would be so easy to forget everything and indulge only in the carnal pleasure she knew this man could give.

As if he knew she was weakening, Simeon brought his mouth down on hers, and, although it was sheer insanity, although it was terribly, terribly wrong, Candra wound her arms round the back of his neck and opened her mouth to his, allowing his tongue to plunder the moist depths, allowing him to take over her body.

CHAPTER TEN

HOW long the kiss lasted, Candra did not know. Whenever Simeon kissed her, time stood still. Her whole body pulsed with love, her need grew, and all hostile thoughts were forgotten. She melted against him, feeling the hard wall of his chest against her breasts, threading her fingers through the wiry thickness of his hair, giving herself freely.

His heart thundered at the same speed as hers, and over and over again he breathed her name, his hands moving over her, moulding her to him, making her a part of him. Candra was lost in a sensual world where time had no meaning and tomorrow never came.

Then a familiar voice shattered their harmony. 'Simeon, are you in there?'

Briony! Candra stiffened and jerked away, wondering what insanity had got into her. Simeon was a married man, for heaven's sake, and here was his wife come searching for him.

'You'd better go,' she said tightly, every word choking her. She felt as though she had been cut in two.

He grimaced, but appeared in no hurry, nor the least bit disturbed that Briony had almost caught them locked in a passionate embrace. 'Tomorrow we must talk,' he said.

Candra shook her head. 'I'm seeing Andrew tomorrow night. We're going looking for fresh moorings. I'm moving my boat.'

'Simeon!' *Four Seasons* moved as Briony stepped

171

on board.

He snorted his impatience. 'I'm coming, Briony.' And Candra wondered how he could treat his new wife so discourteously. 'You're doing yourself no favours, Candra.' He turned his attention back to her.

'I'm doing myself none by remaining here,' she replied smartly.

'I'll see you tomorrow,' he insisted. 'This is absolute nonsense.'

By this time Briony had appeared in the hatchway, trim in tight white jeans and clinging T-shirt. There was a scowl on her face and she said crossly, 'Simeon, I've been calling you for ages. Didn't you hear me?'

He climbed the steps and gave her one of his irresistible smiles, and the next second they had moved out of sight. Candra felt tears sting the backs of her eyelids, but she refused to give way to them. She would not cry over Simeon. He was not worth it. He was a swine, he was a two-timing, smooth-talking bastard. She never wanted to see him again.

She stayed huddled in her cabin, ran the dogs at ten o'clock, and went to bed. Sleep refused to come. She got up at dawn, drank several cups of strong tea, and then drove herself to the office. When everyone else arrived she had already done a couple of hours' work.

Her mother had once told her that work was the panacea for all ills, and for the next few days Candra did not stop. She started early each morning and worked late into the night. Andrew tried to persuade her to take time off to look for moorings, but she refused.

At the end of the week one of the directors asked her if she would consider attending the Group's Annual Conference in Glasgow in his place. 'My wife's not well, I don't want to leave her,' he explained.

Candra jumped at the opportunity. The strain of avoiding Simeon was beginning to tell. It crucified her thinking of him and Briony in the house, and often his bedroom light was on most of the night. The very thought of him holding Briony in his arms, of him kissing Briony, of him making love to her, made Candra feel physically sick. When she came back from Glasgow she would definitely move. It was crazy torturing herself like this.

Although the conference did not begin until Monday afternoon, Candra decided to fly up early on Saturday and spend the weekend exploring the city. She took the dogs to her parents on Friday night, and the next morning packed the few things she would need, turned off the gas, and made sure the boat was securely locked.

When she turned to pick up her case she discovered Simeon standing looking down at it. 'Going somewhere?'

He wore denims and a shirt that needed ironing, and he looked desperately tired. There were thin threads of red in the whites of his eyes and deep shadows beneath. The penalty for staying up most of the night making love, thought Candra bitterly.

But even though she knew he would never be hers she could not quell the leaping of her pulses. Her whole body responded to the male animal in him, and it took every ounce of effort to hide her feelings. She carefully made her tone distant. 'I'm going away on business.'

'For how long?' he frowned.

'A week. I come back next Saturday.'

'Is this a step up your ladder?' His tone was crisp.

Candra shrugged. 'One of the directors' wife is ill,

and he's asked me to take his place.'

'I see.' His blue eyes pierced into hers, making her insides turn to jelly. 'Is Andrew going too?'

'Of course not,' she snapped. Why did he keep harping on about Andrew? Why did it matter to him? And why the hell couldn't she control her feelings?

'How are you getting there? You're surely not driving all that way by yourself?'

And why all these questions? Damn the man, couldn't he see that she wanted him out of her life? 'I'm flying,' she answered shortly, 'and if I don't hurry I shall miss my plane.' Which was a lie. She had hours to spare.

'How about Skye and Lady?'

'My parents are looking after them.'

His frown seemed to deepen with each answer that she gave. 'Are you sure this isn't yet another excuse to avoid me? Don't think I haven't noticed.'

'You surprise me,' she said coldly. 'I thought you'd be far too busy to notice my comings and goings.'

'Candra,' he said with some surprise, 'I don't miss a thing where you're concerned, you should know that.'

'I'm sure Briony wouldn't like to hear you say that.'

'Let's leave Briony out of this,' he snapped.

'Leave her out of it?' her eyes widened. 'When she's the one who's come between us!'

'Only in your mind, Candra.'

She shook her head bewilderedly. 'I don't believe this. You're crazy, absolutely crazy, do you know that?' She snatched up her case and set off at a run towards her car. Simeon followed, and over her shoulder she yelled, 'Perhaps it makes no difference to you, being married, but it makes a hell of a lot of difference to me.'

She rammed the key into the lock and turned it,

throwing her case on the back seat and herself into the front. But Simeon's hand on the door prevented her closing it.

'Do you mind repeating what you just said?'

'You heard,' she rasped, starting the engine and snatching at the gear lever. 'Would you mind getting out of my way? I'm in a hurry.'

'Yes, I damn well would mind,' he returned angrily. 'Candra, you can't go like this without——'

'Can't I?' she grated, letting the clutch pedal out.

'Candra, listen to me, I'm not——'

The car shot forward with a squeal of tyres, drowning his words, slamming the door shut, and in her rear-view mirror she saw his confused and disbelieving face. But she felt no pity for him. Did he expect that, because she felt a strong physical attraction, she would disregard his marriage? Was that what he was prepared to do? She had to admit he did not look happy, but that was nothing to do with her. He had made his proverbial bed and had to lie on it.

She drove furiously all the way to East Midlands Airport, then spent the next two hours walking up and down. There was no doubt in her mind now that she had to move. She did not want to see Simeon Sterne ever again.

The week was full of hectic schedules. Candra was the only female present, and her brain buzzed with information. She had no time to think about Simeon—except in bed at night! Then her mind was full of him. And she knew it would be a long, long time before she got over him, if ever!

Originally a goodbye dinner had been planned at the hotel for Friday evening, but it was suddenly changed.

As most of the men were married and wanted to get back to their wives, it was unanimously agreed that they leave on Friday after their last meeting.

Candra pulled her car on to the drive of Simeon's house shortly before nine, after having first called on her parents to pick up the dogs. She was surprised to see it lined with cars and all the lights on inside the house. Through the windows she could see figures milling around with drinks in their hands.

A party, no less! Probably a belated wedding reception for all the people who had missed out—and organised for a time when he expected her to be away!

She called the dogs to heel and made her way to *Four Seasons* her lips clamped tightly together. The high-powered security light came on as she crossed the lawn, lighting her way, but also making her visible to anyone inside the house who happened to be looking.

After unpacking and changing, she mixed herself a large gin and tonic. She needed it. It was half in her mind to move the boat tonight, but she dismissed the idea as impractical. She would slip silently away first thing in the morning.

As the night was still fairly warm, she took her drink outside. No one could see her from the house, but through the cypress trees she could see tiny pin-points of light. She willed herself to see right through the trees, right through the walls of the house, and right at Simeon himself.

She pictured him in a black dinner suit with a fancy white shirt and a velvet bow-tie, Briony in a silver low-cut dress, hanging on to his arm and his every word, adoration shining in her big violet eyes. She imagined him smiling at Briony, his special smile that Candra had rarely merited, but which said you were the most special person in his life.

Raw jealousy welled in Candra's throat like bile, and she stood up, knocking her chair over as she did so. It clattered noisily against the boat.

She would go in, she would go to bed, she would put a pillow over her ears so that she could not hear the music from the party, or the cars starting up when it was over. She did not want to know.

Then Candra discovered that the dogs were missing. She hoped they hadn't gone to the house. She walked out of the protection of the trees and saw a tall, broad figure making his way towards her. The security light shone brightly in her eyes, so that Candra could not tell who it was, but she knew instinctively that it was Simeon. And he was alone! He had seen her come back and was coming to invite her to the party.

He bent to pat the dogs, and seemed unsure whether to continue, but Candra had no intention of going to him. Eventually he reached her, and it was not until then that Candra saw it was not Simeon after all.

This man was of a similar build, but he had light brown hair and an ugly but fascinating face. 'I hope my dogs weren't being a nuisance,' she said apologetically.

'Not at all. I came out for a breath of air. Boy, is it hot in there.

'I thought you were Simeon.'

He grinned. 'I guess you won't see him for hours. Briony's making sure he doesn't get away. She sure is some girl. Is that your boat? May I take a look? I've always fancied buying a barge.'

'It's a narrow-boat actually,' said Candra coolly. 'Barges are virtually twice as wide and used mainly on rivers.'

'Is that so? I didn't realise.' He stepped on to *Four Seasons* without waiting for her permission, and disappeared inside. Candra had no recourse but to follow.

'This is really something,' he said. 'What's in here? Ah, your bathroom. And this is where you eat. And your kitchen, or do I call it a galley?'

'It doesn't matter,' shrugged Candra. He was being inordinately rude, and yet she could not dislike the man. There was an almost boyish curiosity about him.

Back in the lounge, he flopped into one of the chairs, his legs outstretched. 'You sure are lucky,' he said. 'It's so peaceful here.'

Candra nodded and sat down too.

'Simeon mentioned he had someone living at the bottom of the garden, but he didn't say you were female, or how beautiful you were. What did you say your name was?'

'I didn't, but it's Candra,' she said with a smile.

'And I'm Lance.' He held out his hand and Candra took it. His grip was firm, and it was a long time before he let her go. It should have warned her, but instead she invited him to stay for a drink. This outgoing man was exactly what she needed to take her mind off Simeon.

She poured his lager and another large gin and tonic for herself, and she had no idea how long they sat there talking and drinking. He flirted outrageously, and Candra responded, and when he finally, reluctantly said he must go it came as no surprise when he pulled her into his arms.

She returned his kiss with enthusiasm. She felt light-headed and happier than in a long time, and had even forgotten about Simeon—until he appeared in the end of the boat.

His frown was harsh, his eyes condemning. 'What the hell's going on?'

Lance looked unconcerned. 'It's some girl you've got hidden away here, Simeon.' And he made no attempt to let Candra go.

'And what is that supposed to mean?' Simeon glanced suspiciously from one to the other.

'It means I think she's a beauty,' answered Lance. He gave Candra another quick kiss. 'Perhaps I'll see you again some time, hmm?' And with that he pushed past Simeon and headed back to the house.

Candra had been wrong about the dinner suit. Simeon wore an ordinary lounge suit and tie, and the shadows beneath his eyes had deepened. He had lost weight and looked gaunt, not in the least as though marriage was agreeing with him.

'I didn't expect you back until tomorrow,' he rasped.

'Is that why you had your party tonight?' she asked brittly, and, without waiting for him to answer, added, 'Plans were changed.'

'What was Lance doing here?'

She shrugged. 'He came out for some air and showed an interest in my boat, so——'

'You decided to invite him inside?' His eyes alighted on the empty glasses. 'I'm beginning to wonder whether you were telling me the truth about your career being of more interest than boyfriends. What would have happened, I wonder, if I hadn't come along when I did? Would you have let Lance——'

'Nothing would have happened,' she interrupted him furiously. 'He was just leaving.'

'And that was just an ordinary goodnight kiss?' His eyes blazed into hers. 'It's not what it looked like to me.'

'I don't care what it looked like,' she snapped. 'It meant nothing.'

'To you, maybe not, but Lance looked smitten. I don't think you've seen the last of him.'

Candra felt dismayed, but she firmed her chin and stared at him hostilely. 'He won't be welcome. I'm not interested in him. You'd better tell him that.'

She wished she hadn't poured such large gins. She hadn't eaten since lunch, and then only picked at her food. The gin didn't sit well on an empty stomach. All of a sudden she felt decidedly ill, and put out a hand to steady herself.

Simeon frowned and took her arm. 'Candra, how many drinks have you had?'

'Only a couple, but I haven't eaten, and——'

He swore beneath his breath. 'What stupidity. You'd better lie down. I must return to my guests, but they're on the verge of going. I'll be back.'

'No.' Candra shook her head, then wished she hadn't. 'I'll be all right. I don't need you.'

'I think you do,' he said, propelling her firmly along to her bedroom, watching as she lay down on top of the covers.

How about Briony? she wanted to ask. I can't see her letting you come here. But she felt too ill to bother.

When he had gone, Candra closed her eyes and felt the cabin whirling around her. She felt nauseous now, as well, and wondered whether she ought to go to the bathroom.

She was still thinking about it when Simeon returned. Her first indication that he was here was the rocking of the boat as he stepped on board. It felt like a gigantic wave had hit it, and she put her hand to her head to stop the dizziness.

Next she heard him filling the kettle, then he came to her and stood looking sternly down. He had taken off the jacket to his suit, and his sleeves were rolled up workmanlike. 'Still feeling lousy?'

'Yes,' she admitted.

'It was a stupid thing to do.'

'You don't have to tell me.' She hauled herself into a sitting position, her back resting against the wall at the head of the bed. 'And you don't have to look after me. I'm quite capable of looking after myself.'

'So it seems,' he clipped drily. 'How many times have you done this sort of thing before?'

'Never.'

'Yet you chose a complete stranger to get drunk with? I find that very odd.'

'I had no intention of getting drunk,' she snapped.

'But you must have offered Lance a drink.'

'So what?' Candra's eyes blazed angrily.

'You were taking a chance. I'm glad I came along when I did. You seemed to be giving yourself pretty freely, and one cannot help but wonder what might have happened if you hadn't been disturbed.'

Candra had wondered the same thing, but she didn't take kindly to Simeon's voicing her own thoughts. 'Hadn't you better go and see to the kettle?' she asked coldly.

She closed her eyes after he had gone, wishing he hadn't come back, wishing he hadn't seen her like this. It was too degrading. But it was his fault. If he hadn't had his damned party to celebrate his damned wedding, she wouldn't have felt compelled to drink.

He returned with a mug of black coffee and a plate of lightly buttered toast. Candra groaned at the mere thought of food. 'I can't eat that.'

'You're going to,' he insisted, and he stood over her while she ate every crumb and sipped the coffee until the mug was empty, and she had to admit that afterwards she felt slightly better.

But she still did not like the humiliation of him seeing her, and when he appeared in no hurry to leave she said crossly, 'Don't you think you ought to go? Won't Briony be wondering what's happened to you?'

'Briony knows where I am.'

'You told her?' she asked incredulously.

'Not that you were drunk,' he assured her with a smile. 'But that you were ill and needed looking after.'

'And she didn't mind?'

His smile widened. 'Briony can be very understanding.'

'That I don't believe,' snapped Candra. 'But you needn't stay any longer. I'm all right now. Go back to you beloved wife before she comes after you.'

'I don't think there's any fear of that.' He grinned. 'She's probably already tucked up in bed.'

Waiting for him! Candra closed her eyes, refusing to let him see her pain, and wondering why he found it all so amusing. 'You can still go.'

'I don't think I ought to leave you just yet.'

Her eyes shot open as she felt him sit down on the edge of the bed. 'Simeon, what the hell do you think you're doing?'

'Keeping my eye on you.'

'I've told you, I don't need you.'

'I think you do,' he said quietly.

And he was right. She needed him desperately, she wanted him, hungered for him, but he belonged to someone else and all such thoughts had to be squashed. She would never be free of him, though. She was fated to be trapped by her love forever.

'I shall stay here until I'm satisfied that you're better.'

'If you went I could sleep,' she said crossly.

'What's stopping you? Close your eyes, go to sleep, I promise not to disturb you.'

Didn't he know he was doing that simply by being here? 'You're impossible,' she cried. 'You tell me off about inviting Lance in, you don't like Andrew here either, and yet you see nothing wrong in sitting in my bedroom yourself.'

'I care deeply for you, Candra. I would never do you any harm, you should know that.'

But not deeply enough to stop him marrying Briony. Her eyes flashed angrily. 'I don't care what you think about me, if you were a gentleman you'd leave when I ask.' Her breasts heaved as she fought for control. How could she hide this love of hers when it consumed every inch of her? When she could feel the warmth of him, and his maleness, and her body cried out for fulfilment? She wanted to reach out and touch him. She wanted him in bed with her. Oh, lord, how she wanted him.

'I'd leave if I thought it was what you really wanted,' he said softly, 'but somehow I don't think you do. I think you're using words to fight what is going on inside you.'

His blue eyes held hers for several long seconds, and Candra groaned and then began to speak. It was as though he were forcing the words out of her. She did not want to say them, but could not help herself. 'You know very well I want you to make love to me, but how can I let you when Briony's waiting up at the house? Oh, why did you marry her? I can see you're not happy. You don't love her and she doesn't love you, not the way you deserve to be loved, not the way I love you.'

The words were out before she could stop them, and Candra immediately covered her face with her hands. 'Forget I said that, Simeon. Forget everything. Just go, please go. I can't take any more of this.' Unbidden tears forced themselves from between her closed lids and she turned away from him and buried her face in the pillow.

She felt his hand on her shoulder, gently persuading her to look at him, but she shrugged him off. 'Don't, Simeon.'

'There's something I have to tell you, Candra,' he said softly.

'Nothing you can say will make any difference,' she whimpered, knowing she was making an even greater fool of herself.

'I think this will.' He paused a moment, then went on, 'I'm not married to Briony.'

There was a second's absolute stillness as his words sank in, then slowly, hesitantly, Candra turned. Her eyes were wide and tears trembled and spilled. 'I don't understand,' she whispered. 'You're—not—married?'

He smiled and shook his head, and the tenderness in his eyes crucified Candra.

'But——' She swallowed painfully. 'But—Briony told me herself. She—she said you were getting married in New York.'

He swore beneath his breath, but his smile was gentle. 'I'm afraid it was all wishful thinking on her part. I know she wants to marry me, and at one time I did think of it, but that was before I met you. From the moment you came into my office spitting fire, I knew that you were the one for me.'

'You did?' Candra's beautiful eyes grew even wider.

'But you were a dedicated career woman, determined never to lose your heart to any man. I feared I would never win you.' He took a handkerchief from his pocket and gently mopped her cheeks.

She caught his hand and held it against her face. 'I admit I tried my hardest to fight what I felt for you, Simeon, but it was impossible. I love you so much it hurts.' Fresh tears filled her eyes, but this time they were of happiness.

'And yet you stopped me making love to you.'

'I had to, for my own sanity. I thought you—I didn't know—oh, Simeon, I'm sorry. I think I hurt myself as much you. It was the worst night I've ever spent.'

'Me too,' he growled.

'Would you really have never touched me again?'

He nodded. 'Though goodness knows it was hard. I've hardly had a night's sleep thinking of you down here and me up there, wishing you were in my bed.'

'And I thought you were with Briony.'

He smiled ruefully. 'I could kill that girl. But I knew you had to make up your own mind. I didn't want to influence you. I thought if I let my eyes tell you how I felt, my body language, then if you felt anything for me at all you would come to me in your own good time. I didn't count on Briony putting her oar in. I'm sorry she said what she did. She had no right.'

'She was jealous, I suppose.'

'As hell,' he agreed. 'But I told her tonight that if I couldn't marry you I would marry no one. And boy, was she shocked. Apparently she was hoping to announce our engagement tonight; the party was all her idea. She went off feeling very sorry for herself, and somehow I don't think we shall be seeing very much of her in future.'

'Oh, Simeon.' Candra trembled as he gathered her into his arms.

'I love you so very much, my darling,' he said. 'I'll never let anyone hurt you again.'

She lifted her mouth to his, and the two dogs came in to her bedroom to see what was going on.

'When did you find out that you loved me?' he asked gently, when they finally drew apart for breath.

'When I stopped hating you,' she smiled. 'I really did hate you in the beginning. I saw red when I knew what you wanted to do with my grandfather's land.'

'Do you still object?'

She shook her head. 'I realise that you're giving Stonely what it wants, and I have to admit reluctantly that you're making a good job of it. It won't be the eyesore I first thought.'

'We've also overcome our problems with the marina,' he said. 'It won't be long before that's finished, too.'

'I thought you were a monster for moving us all when we were so happy,' she told him, trying to look stern but failing completely.

'No one objected as much as you.'

She shrugged. 'It didn't matter to most of them where they lived. Just me and George. I thought you treated him diabolically. If it hadn't been for his son finding out about that cottage he would have been——'

'You mean *my* cottage?' he interrupted with a twinkle

in his eyes.

Candra frowned. 'What do you mean?'

'I bought it.'

'*You* bought it? *You* were the one who paid that horrendous price?'

He nodded.

'I don't believe it,' she said. 'I enquired after the cottage myself, thinking George could sell his boat and buy it. But not at that price. You must be mad! But I love you for doing it, and I don't deserve you. I really have thought the worst of you. Oh, Simeon, will you ever forgive me?'

'There's nothing to forgive.' He smiled indulgently. 'I didn't exactly treat you very fairly myself. But how do you treat a girl who's as prickly as a porcupine and refuses to let you anywhere near?'

'Oh, Simeon.' Candra wound her arms around him and he lay down beside her. The two dogs rested their noses on the edge of the bed and watched them kissing.

'We'll get married as soon as I can get a licence,' said Simeon eventually. 'I've sold my town house, and I'm negotiating to buy my friend's lovely place here. We'll honeymoon on this boat. We'll take it away and we'll lose ourselves. We'll forget about work and careers and concentrate on the more important things in life like making love and making babies and making each other happy.'

'I am happy,' said Candra, her eyes shining. 'I never thought I could be so happy. I never knew that there were men like you about. Oh, Simeon, I love you with all my heart.'

'I love you too, my darling. I don't think I'm going to have the strength of mind to leave you tonight and go back to the house.'

'You don't have to,' she whispered softly.

'You won't reject me again?'

She shook her head, her eyes shining with her love for this man. She was trapped no longer. She was as free as a bird, free to love, free to feel every emotion, free to express herself in any way she wished. She was confident, too, that Simeon would never hurt her as her father had, as Craig had. He would treat her always with gentleness and consideration. He was the man she had been looking for and never expected to find.

'I'm so lucky,' she whispered.

He smiled. 'That makes two of us.'

Zodiac Wordsearch
Competition

How would you like a years supply of Mills & Boon Romances ABSOLUTELY FREE?

Well, you can win them! All you have to do is complete the word puzzle below and send it into us by Dec 31st 1990. The first five correct entries picked out of the bag after this date will each win a years supply of Mills & Boon Romances (Six books every month - worth over £100!) What could be easier?

S	E	C	S	I	P	R	I	A	M	F
I	U	L	C	A	N	C	E	R	L	I
S	A	I	N	I	M	E	G	N	S	R
C	A	P	R	I	C	O	R	N	U	E
S	E	I	R	A	N	G	I	S	I	O
Z	O	D	W	A	T	E	R	B	R	I
O	G	A	H	M	A	T	O	O	A	P
D	R	R	T	O	U	N	I	R	U	R
I	I	B	R	O	R	O	M	G	Q	O
A	V	I	A	N	U	A	N	C	A	C
C	E	L	E	O	S	T	A	R	S	S

Pisces	Aries	Leo	Earth	**Please turn over for entry details**
Cancer	Gemini	Virgo	Star	
Scorpio	Taurus	Fire	Sign	
Aquarius	Libra	Water	Moon	
Capricorn	Sagittarius	Zodiac	Air	

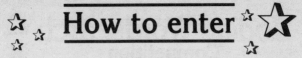

☆ How to enter ☆

All the words listed overleaf, below the word puzzle, are hidden in the grid. You can can find them by reading the letters forwards, backwards, up and down, or diagonally. When you find a word, circle it, or put a line through it. After you have found all the words, the left-over letters will spell a secret message that you can read from left to right, from the top of the puzzle through to the bottom.

Don't forget to fill in your name and address in the space provided and pop this page in an envelope (you don't need a stamp) and post it today.   Competition closes Dec 31st 1990.

Only one entry per household (more than one will render the entry invalid).

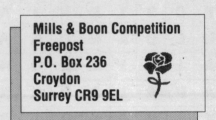

Mills & Boon Competition
Freepost
P.O. Box 236
Croydon
Surrey CR9 9EL

Hidden message _____

_____

Are you a Reader Service subscriber.   Yes ❑   No ❑

Name_____

Address_____

_____

_____

_____**Postcode**_____

You may be mailed with other offers as a result of entering this competition.
If you would prefer not to be mailed please tick the box. No ❑   COMP9